WHEN
YOUR LOVER
LEAVES

Also available in Perennial Library
by Susan Trott:

Don't Tell Laura
The Housewife and the Assassin
Incognito

WHEN
YOUR LOVER
LEAVES

Susan Trott

Harper & Row, Publishers, New York
Cambridge, Philadelphia, San Francisco, Washington
London, Mexico City, São Paulo, Singapore, Sydney

A hardcover edition of this book was originally published in Great Britain in 1980 by Severn House Publishers, Ltd. and in the United States by St. Martin's Press. It is here reprinted by arrangement with Jonathan Dolger Agency.

Library of Congress Cataloging-in-Publication Data

Trott, Susan.
    When your lover leaves.
    I. Title.
[PS3570.R594W48   1987]   813'.54   86-46233
ISBN 0-06-097107-X (pbk.)

87 88 89 90 91 92 MPC 10 9 8 7 6 5 4 3 2 1

for my daughters, Ann and Natalie

Contents

When your lover leaves   1

Your body grieves   41

Running   59

And gasping   85

You try to prevail   109

Utterly raped   145

And threatened with jail   187

You become   193

The lone-juicing, uncowed runner-of-mountains,
Female   209

When Your
Lover Leaves

1 ...

C hard and onions. That seemed to be all my
garden was yielding now in the advanced stages
of the autumn season. With the harvest of chard in my arms,
I stood pondering the depleted rows. I doubted that the last
tomatoes were going to ripen. There simply wasn't enough
sun—even though tomatoes redden at night. As for the
zucchinis, they kept bravely bursting out with big yellow
blooms but the vegetables that resulted from them were
pitiful. The burgeoning squash would become arrested in
its development like a man going through an impotent
period.

Was there such a thing as chard and onion soup, I
wondered, for I was in the soup business. I don't see why
there mightn't as well be. I think there is about to be. I had
that chicken stock. I'd add the onions, sautéed first in butter, and the chard at the last along with ... hmmm, some
very thin egg noodles, why not? Sounds good. Sounds damn
good.

I carried the vegetables to the kitchen sink, and there
was Joe! "I didn't hear you arrive. You're home early."

I emptied my arms of produce and threw them around

Joe, being careful not to touch his lovely business suit with my earthy hands.

"I wanted to come home early since we wouldn't be dining together tonight."

"That's right. It's Gramps' Night." On Thursday Gramps came to dinner and Joe took his sons out. "Just wait until I wash my hands so I can hug you properly."

"I'll get out of my clothes so you can hug me properly."

"I'll wash my hands and get out of my clothes and into bed so I can hug you properly."

We hugged improperly, a clarion coition. What a happy time. Afterward we lay peacefully on the old oaken bed in the small yellow bedroom. Impulsive in our passion, I had not drawn the curtains, and I could see the day softening into dusk. I cudgeled my brain for some line of poetry to quote to Joe about the dusk, but then I was afraid to speak it lest dusk make him think of dust. I hadn't gotten around to much housekeeping that day. Joe was used to servants in his other life that he had only recently abandoned for good. Dust was one of the difficulties he was experiencing in living with me. The other difficulties were the smallness of my house, my old dog who smelled, and my cat who was mean.

So I said nothing about dusk and anyhow it was nice to lie together in the silent aftermath of love. Presently Joe reached over for his clarinet, which he kept in a case by the bed, and he tootled away on it for a time before getting up out of bed to really address himself to the instrument. He played "Autumn Leaves."

It was inexpressibly sweet-sounding. Pure honey. He stood by the yellow wall, a tall, naked man with beautiful arms and hands, playing the clarinet. On the wall nearby was an early Diego Rivera watercolor of a white cow standing disconsolately by a tree. I will hold in my mind's eye forever that picture of Joe, the clarinet, and the cow—and forever in my mind's ear the sound of that sad song of ending.

There were tears in my eyes when the song was done.

"Thank you. That was beautiful. Thank you, Joe, for being so good to me."

"I love you with all my heart," he said simply. "I have never been so happy."

"I'm so glad. I want to make you even happier. What can I do?"

"Nothing. You are perfect."

He sat down on the bed and fell to kissing me all over. Joe loved to kiss. As did I. We turned ourselves inside out to please each other. Joe entered me and rested there inside me, large and hard. He liked to do that, just be there inside me, not moving, remaining enormous. He could stay like that upward of an hour. It was quite an experience.

I had to remind him of Gramps' Night. Alas.

2 . . .

*I*f only Gramps' Night were all it sounded. It had begun that way, with Gramps coming for dinner once a week. Then one time he brought a friend. And then another friend. And the friends brought friends. Since I was in the soup business, there was always plenty of soup in the big army pots upon my six-burner stove. Finally there got to be so many old people I didn't have the bowls. That was okay; they'd bring their own. And spoons too.

They always got dolled up. It was their evening out. It became a big social event. It was good food and it was free. This little town had a lot of old people in it, and their pensions didn't keep up with inflation. As well, the rising property taxes on their houses did not reflect the rocklike immutability of their incomes.

So the word spread. Finally there were so many that I split them up into two nights. Two Gramps' Nights, Monday and Thursday. Well, what happened then was that they all came both nights. Joe didn't know that it had gotten up to two nights. He'd been away a couple of weeks on business for Wells Fargo Bank, where he worked. This was Thursday Gramps' Night; I figured I'd tell Joe about Monday when it came.

Joe went off to collect his sons, and I put the flames on under the minestrone and the chicken soup, adding some water to both pots.

The old people came, but I won't go into a lot of detail about it. They came. The air rang with their voices and was redolent of that bittersweet smell that old people have, overlaid with aroma of soups.

There were twenty-five of us in all. My house was small, but I had picnic tables and benches out in the yard which would do until the rains came, and then I didn't see why we couldn't put up a tent of some sort.

They brought baked goods for dessert. There were always pies and cobblers and cakes, and everyone made a big fuss about how good they were, which was part of the pleasure of the whole thing. Gramps' Night was always a party. Everyone got to talk about their diseases. I'd say about three-fourths of the old people had been operated on, or were being treated for, cancer.

It was good that they could talk about it. Think what a dark, bitter, malignant secret it used to be. That was another great thing about Gramps—how he'd haul in some lonely crotchety person who'd sit there all resentful, damned if he was going to say a word to anyone or accept any charity. Then the weeks would go by and he'd be shouting along with the rest of them and also bringing a contribution of cookies or flowers or whatever. Some of them had vegetable patches too, and they'd bring along stuff for some future soup. In short, Gramps' Night was a grand affair.

3 . . .

*I*t wasn't until everyone had gone and I was cleaning up that I looked into the soup pots to assess the remains and saw that they were empty! I had soup deliveries to make to two restaurants the next day—Splashing Waters where my best friend, Maude, was lunch waitress, and Le Fromage. The Splash and The Cheese, as I called them, were my best customers. For the rest I catered private citizens. Well, I would just have to get going on the chard and onion soup. But I felt exhausted. Actually, since the whole key to the soup was adding things at the last, I could wait until morning, get up a little earlier.

"What do you think, Moby?" I asked my cat. Moby, cleaning himself up from his latest fracas, looked dubious. Blue, my beloved old poodle-Labrador, who was always in the same room I was and always on my wavelength, looked sympathetic about my fatigue but suggested that I at least sauté the onions.

So I was slicing onions and weeping accordingly when Joe arrived home. I couldn't see him very well through my tears, but I lifted my face for him to kiss, unable to hug him for the second time that day because of my hands. Did he seem to hesitate a second before leaning down to kiss me?

"What's this? Why are you working at this hour?"

"Soup's all gone. I've got to get started on a new one."

"Your soup business is not going to be a success, Ronda."

"It's not?" said I, amazed. It was unlike Joe to say a negative thing to me. "Whatever do you mean?"

"Your Gramps' Night has gotten out of hand. They're eating up your profits . . . if you *have* any profits."

"Why, Joe . . ." I began scrubbing my hands so I could release myself from the onions and give him all my attention.

"Here you finally found something you could do well and make money at, and you're blowing it. You were a complete success, filling a need in the town, until the expanding Gramps' Night . . ."

"They contribute . . ."

"To the meal, yes, but not to your soup."

"Sometimes to my soup."

"A potato here, a carrot there. Also, since we're on the subject, you've been thinning your soups. They're not as good. You've been thinning your soups to make them stretch."

I blushed. Only a few hours before I had added water to both my soups. It was a culinary crime. He was right to mention it. I'd been doing it behind my own back, as it were.

He had every right to be saying these things. When I first met Joe, I was a widow lady, barely making it, trying to support myself and my son, Sam. I had death benefits from the National Park Service amounting to eight thousand a year, to which I would sometimes add a thousand or two from selling short stories (for I am a dedicated fictionist). But I found that I was unable to hold down a proper job for more than a couple of months. I was an incompetent. I simply could not keep my mind on what I was doing and would make grievous errors. My bosses let me go gently, but with what I could only perceive to be genuine relief.

It was Joe who brainstormed with me to find out what I could do well. I was a good mother, I said, a good creative writer, and a really good soup builder.

My mothering had no monetary value. I did what I could with my short stories but there wasn't a big market for short fiction in this country. I would sell in other countries but it would be a hundred dollars here, seventy-five dollars there. "If only I could capitalize on the fact that I look exactly like Virginia Woolf," I told Joe.

"I didn't know that you did."

"Oh yes; people often remark on it." I got out the Quentin Bell biography and showed him the picture on the cover, the one on the back where she's older and crazier.

"So you do," he agreed. "But I think your money's to be found in soup."

So we went for the soup. And it was a smash success. For the first time since my husband died four years ago, I was sitting pretty. Sitting pretty isn't important to me. Getting by is fine. Providing just enough money for me and Sam to live simply and to get him educated is fine with me. "The man who knows what enough is," said Lao Tsu, "will always have enough." Still, I was perfectly willing to free myself and Sam from want and to sit as pretty as the next man. And so I sat until, as Joe pointed out, the ever-expanding Gramps' Night.

Wait until he heard about number two Gramps' Night! Or about my catering service.

My private-party soup service got poleaxed when Joe started living openly with me. Many of the upper crust were friends of the Mastersons and they wished to show their disapproval—or, who knows, maybe Louise Masterson, Joe's wife, put out the word that Ronda's Soup Service guaranteed all-out indigestion.

Anyhow, something happened. But I never mentioned it to Joe. I figured the business would right itself. Meanwhile I was holding my own. I didn't want to be any financial drain on Joe. Sam was willing to get a job bussing dishes down at U.C. San Diego, but I didn't want him to do that. I wanted him to study.

So Joe had every right to say these things, yet it was unlike him. For him it almost amounted to an attack. Always the encourager, he was not a man to enjoy finding fault.

I washed my hands, put the onions behind me, and drew Joe into the little living room furnished with a fire-place, studio couch, straight-back chair, and books.

"No, don't build a fire," he said, seeing me go for the kindling. It always seemed to me that conversation had to be complemented by a fire.

"Oh ... all right." I was thrown off. Joe was always

tolerant of my fire-building. Now that my eyes were cleared of the onion-induced tears, I could see that he looked as strange as he was acting. His intelligent face with the gentle blue eyes looked stricken. I felt alarmed. "Joe!"

He began to talk. But it was not about soup. Not at all.

"I'm going back to Louise," he said.

I was staggered. I was standing at the time, by the wood box, and I literally fell back as if stunned by a blow, almost losing my footing. He took hold of me and sat me down on the couch, but I stood up again.

"Because of the soup?" I asked.

"What?"

"Because I'm failing at the soup business?"

"No, no. That has nothing to do with it. I don't know why I got started on that. I'm sorry."

"Sorry? Sorry about saying that? What about this? What about saying you're going back to Louise? It can't be true, Joe. You didn't really say that?"

"It is true."

"It's always hard for you to come back to this little house, Joe, after an evening with your sons and after being awhile in your gorgeous mansion, remembering how very comfortable your life was. I appreciate how hard that is. I know that in many ways my life is antipathetical to your nature, but once . . ."

Once we fulfill our dream, I was about to say. We had a dream of living as artists together, me writing, Joe devoting himself to his music. We had a dream of writing a musical together, Joe composing, I the lyricist. As it was, my house was too small even to contain his grand piano. But it would only be a few years before our children were educated; then Joe could quit the bank, my soup business would be thriving . . .

Oh God, my poor soup business. Well, I'd cancel out that second Gramps' Night and . . .

"It hasn't anything to do with houses, Ronda. It's because Louise asked me, begged me to return. She's gone into a decline since I left. She can't cope. She was more dependent on me than she knew. She and the children need me. It's the right thing."

"But what about us? Our love? Isn't that the right thing?"

"It's perfect," he said sadly.

"I must have done something wrong."

"Nothing."

"I've disappointed you in some way. Please tell me."

"You're wonderful. You're the most wonderful woman I've ever known. It hasn't to do with you or with us. I simply have to do the right thing or I can't live with myself."

I knew this was true. He was a responsible person, a gentleman. And yet . . . There was something he was not telling me. There had to be. Feeling weak, I sat down on the couch.

"Did you have dinner with her tonight instead of your boys?"

"Yes. She'd asked me if we could talk. I didn't want to tell you and upset you. I didn't know it was going to be so serious." He held up his hand to ward off any questions. He never talked about Louise to me and I tried to respect his prudence.

After a heavy silence I said in a small voice, "It's true? You're really going back to her?"

"It's true."

"Then there's nothing more to say." From some mysterious place in my being came a superb dignity to help me through the coming hour. "I'll just take Blue for a walk while you remove your things. So I don't have to watch." I rose unsteadily to my feet.

"Ronda . . ."

"Don't touch me, Joe." He'd made a tender gesture toward me. "Please don't call me in the days to come. Don't call me to see how I am. I will need *not* to hear your voice. That is my wish. Please honor it."

"I will." He stood with his hands by his sides, his head

hanging. It was an alien posture for Joe. Suddenly his face crumpled; he wept. Silent tears streamed from his eyes into arroyos of wrinkles I'd never seen before.

"Come, Blue," I said, going out the door into the black night that had emerged from the soft silent dusky aftermath of our love only hours before—emerged from where it had concealed itself.

Off we went, Blue and I, into the dark night of the soul.

4 . . .

A few nights later I drove up to Joe's house to see if his car was there, which would mean he was there, which would verify the fact that he'd gone back to his wife. Because maybe he hadn't. Maybe I'd gotten it all wrong. But his car was there all right. It was there in the carport next to Louise's car, next to the somber, stone house.

I visualized him in bed with Louise. I visualized him making love to her and knew he wouldn't be able to for some time. I'll grant him that much sensibility, even though he'd said he'd go back to her only hours after our happy time in the oaken bed.

No, he could not go blithely from my body to hers. I knew that for sure as I pondered his brooding house.

Suddenly I wanted to do something to make my presence known. Why not write a note, tie it to a rock, throw it through their bedroom window? I could say something pungent and profound. Louise would call the police. I imagined her the sort of woman who would call the police right away, even before she read the note. They would come to apprehend me and I would run from them, being such a very fast runner. No, better to let them grab me. Then Joe would have to decide whether to press charges. Better to let them seize me and drag me away before his pain-filled eyes.

But what would the note say?

Unable to compose a stirring note, I left the scene and, in any case, as it turned out, I was stopped by a policeman in a patrol car on the way home. He thought that I was drunk but was soon disembarrassed of that notion when he saw that it was me. I have almost always lived in this town and am known for my sobriety. This policeman and I had gone to school together. His name was Mack Scher and he was my friend and neighbor.

He gave me a handkerchief. "You shouldn't drive and cry at the same time," he said. "You were weaving all over the road."

"You guys better get some sort of inhalator that can detect the tear level in people. We criers are a menace on the roads."

He observed me quietly. "This road you're coming down goes up to Joe Masterson's house."

"It goes up to a lot of people's houses."

Mack knew that Joe had left me and so he said, "Don't do anything crazy, Ronda."

"Who, me?"

"Yeah, you. You're one of those nice quiet people who all of a sudden does something crazy. You don't care."

"On the contrary, I care too much."

"But you don't care what people think, which, if you did, would act as a deterrent—along with the law, of course."

"May I go home now, officer?"

"Can I have my handkerchief back?"

"Let me wash it for you; it's got snot all over it." I put my Honda in gear, then it occurred to me to ask, "What are you doing up this way, Mack?"

"I'm going to talk to the woman who got raped the other night. She wasn't in much of a condition to talk at the time."

"Raped! A woman here in town got raped?"

"I wish you read the papers."

"Was it the County Rapist?"

"Looks like it."

"Poor woman." I forgot my own troubles for a minute, then I combined her troubles with mine, seemed to make a connection. "Was it Louise? Was the raped woman Louise Masterson? That would explain everything, Mack. Everything!"

"You know I can't say who she was. We have to promise, uh . . . confidentiality."

"But Mack," I wailed, "it would help me so much to know. I would understand then. It's so hard not to understand about Joe leaving me. You could at least tell me if it's *not* her."

"But if I couldn't tell you it wasn't, it would be telling that it was."

I began to cry again and to apply the sodden handkerchief.

"Okay, for Christ's sake. Jee-sus. All right. It wasn't her."

"Honest?"

"Honest. Now go home and stay there."

I drove on home, my mind whirling. To have some neighbor raped would scare you badly, I thought. It would certainly make you wish you had a man in the house for protection. A near neighbor raped . . . maybe it was a friend . . . that could scare Louise into begging Joe to come back. It scared me just to have the Rapist in the town. With no man in the house. No man . . .

I realized that for the first time in my life I was living alone. I'd gone right from my family to my marriage with Alan Thompson, and Sam was thirteen when Alan was killed. It was a freak accident. He was struck on the head by a rock, part of a small avalanche, while hiking up the Yosemite Falls trail on a rescue. They booted me out of the ranger's house we had lived in in the park, so I returned to

... 13

my home town and dedicated myself to Sam until I began
with Joe, three years later.

I'd known Joe at a distance, since he and his wife were
prominent in the town and he had been the town mayor for
the last two years. It was only when we chanced to run
together one day that we began to grow close. He was hiking
with a group of friends on the mountain that embraced our
town. I was running alone. For some reason he decided to
run a little way with me. We fell in beside each other in such
a natural, pleasurable way. We ran, step for step, breath for
breath, exchanged surprising intimacies—our first intercourse.

A year later he moved in with me, just after my beloved
Sam left for college. Joe and I lived together fewer than
three months.

So I'd never been alone in all my thirty-five years.

I remembered talks I'd had with friends· and women
acquaintances, many of whom had suffered intolerable
marital situations, but who would not leave their husbands.
There was the fear of financial insecurity, of course, and of
coming down in the world to a smaller house or apartment,
but stronger than that was the fear of loneliness, which, I
was given to understand, begins to be a very big fear as you
get older.

"You want someone in the rocking chair next to
you."

"Not if you hate that person, surely."

"Yes, even then. I'd rather have someone to fight with
than no one."

"Not me," I bragged. "I'll opt for the empty rocker. I'd
rather be alone with me, who I like and who amuses me,
than with a person I find repugnant. And I want always to
operate on true feeling."

"There's no such thing as love," Maude said. "There
are only needs, dependencies, bonds."

"I disdain those things," I said. "I have nothing but
scorn for people who are lonely or scared."

Brave words! Spoken by one who, at the time, was secure in the knowledge that she was beloved.

As I got out of my car, I resolved not to succumb to loneliness or fear. If I wake in the night, scared and lonely, I will shout aloud, "I scorn you!" Meaning me for having those feelings. Meaning old age and death and rapists. I will shout them away, shout them off my breast and shoulders where they, loneliness and fear, will try to cling to me, exhaling their fetid breath.

I went into the house and closed the door behind me.

I'm alone now, I thought. I must get into a whole new way of thinking, feeling, and being that isn't connected with Joe, that isn't identifying myself with him. It will probably take a little while.

5 . . .

I went to town the next day to practice being alone. I walked in and out of shops, talking to people. I went hither and yon: to the library for books, to Paradise Produce for pinto beans, to the bus depot for a piece of carrot cake to eat on the spot, to the police station to leave the clean-washed handkerchief for Mack. I could have left it at his apartment, which was across the street from me, but since he had given it to me in the line of duty, I didn't.

I practiced going about town, walking and talking, a lone woman, no longer connected with Joe or with anyone, no longer needing Joe or anyone. I guess I wanted to show the town, and myself, that I was all right, even though I was not all right, because if I were, would I have gone walking and talking around the town for no reason in such a dumb-ass way, acting so totally out of character?

I had a vision of making this obsessive round every day

from now on, becoming thereby some sort of pitiful town peculiar: the woman who walks and talks through town.

"She's been that way since her lover left. She was a private sort of person before, a nice widow lady who lived quietly with her son, wrote stories I think, although they're not in any books. Then she upped and had this wild affair with Joe Masterson, who lives in the big stone house up on the hill. Vee Pee at Wells Fargo and the town mayor to boot! Left his wife he did. Smitten he was. Moved right in with Mrs. Thompson for the whole town to see. Then, before we could take that all in, he'd gone back to his wife and family. Since then Mrs. Thompson comes daily to town, goes into every shop and out again, collars people, talks. You can tell time by her comings and goings. Let's see, 3:05 P.M. That'll put her at the bus depot, I think. No. Nope, she'll be at Splashing Waters, talking to Maude. That's when Maude finishes up."

My friend Maude finished up her lunch waitressing at The Splash around three o'clock. I found her sitting at a table counting bills and coins and putting them in a money box. Although Maude was a tall, stunning redhead, her beauty was not of a waitressy kind; it was more along the lines of an aristocrat. She was one of those gutsy women who did leave an intolerable marital situation even if it meant becoming a waitress in her own town in a place that was more of a lowlife bar than your nice ladies' luncheon restaurant. The Splash only served lunch to give itself a respectable air before its nightly descent into hell.

It was a good place by day, not Hemingway's Clean Well Lighted Place, but fairly clean and lit by the sun, a large high-ceilinged space with a fine collection of old oak tables and chairs.

After the owner hired her he fell into despair because

she never smiled at his customers. He couldn't get her to smile either but he couldn't bring himself to fire her because she added such tone to the place and he really hungered after tone.

Maude, too, was a runner, but she had the long, lean, racy look of the distance runner, whereas I had the more sensuous fleshy look of the recent erotic adventurer. I was running fifty-mile weeks but when Joe moved in I slipped back to more like twenty-five.

I'd known Maude for twenty-one years. She moved to our town when we were both fourteen years old. We met the summer before freshman year when we both had jobs at the variety store. There the customers called us Miss, and we've called each other that to this day. Maude got good grades in school, better than I did, because even then all I wanted to do was read and write stories. Maude was also much more popular with boys than me, being so beautiful, but I didn't care; I was in a dream world much of the time. There was no one I liked or wanted to be liked by, until I met Alan the summer after my graduation.

"How are you doing, Miss?" she asked as I sat down.

"Not very well. It's so hard. It's so hard to understand."

"I'm going to talk to him myself," said Maude. "I want to understand it too. You were so completely happy, you two. It doesn't make sense. You made me believe in love for a while there."

"It sounds funny but I keep thinking it has something to do with the Rapist—because someone was raped up there by Joe's house only the night before he left me."

"Louise?"

"No, but the fear of rape is as bad as rape itself. Loneliness is fear, and women's greatest fear is rape."

"But why should he go back to her just because she's scared? And why wouldn't he worry about *you* being alone?"

"I don't know."

"I'm scared of the Rapist too," said Maude.

"I'm terrified," I confessed.

"He likes younger women."

"I'm afraid I look young at a distance. I'm going to put a sign in the window saying I'm thirty-five."

Maude snickered.

The bartender sent over a glass of white wine for Maude and juice for me. I raised my glass and made my big announcement.

"I've decided to train for a marathon."

"Hmph," said Maude. This is about as far as she'll ever go to show surprise but it's nevertheless entirely gratifying.

"I know I said I never would. I was going to be a contented middle distance runner, but heck . . ."

"It's like your story."

"What story?"

"The one you wrote about six or eight months ago. A lady lost her lover and decided to train for a marathon instead of committing suicide."

"God, that's right. That is really spooky because I am beginning to realize that my stories predict my life. I not only draw from my past and present but from my future. It's a whole new literary form: precognitive fiction. Like these last few months I've been doing a deep study of St. Francis and I recently realized that my first published story—it was in *MLLE*, *years* ago—was about a young man who had been studying St. Francis and then began to believe that he was St. Francis. I wonder," I said seriously, "if I think I'm St. Francis. Do you think I am?"

"No, I do not."

"That's good. I would like to be like him, though, if I could: gentle, courteous, benevolent. Of course he was informed by God. I don't believe in God but I do believe one can learn how to live from people like St. Francis, and Jesus, and Karol Wojtyla."

"Okay, Miss. On to more important things. What marathon are you going to run?"

"You mean I have to name one? I thought the great thing about training for a marathon is that you could do it indefinitely without ever necessarily having to run one."

"Well, you were wrong. Sorry." She closed the cashbox decisively and said, "Avenue of the Giants. Early in May. That'll give you four months to train."

"Okay. Will you come too? And run?"

"Of course."

6 . . .

When I got back home, Blue and Moby were both waiting for me at the gate of my picket fence, as if they were making a point of helping me through this first week alone without Joe. It warmed my heart. In the mail was a letter from my brother in New York, about Joe leaving me, for I had called and told him the next morning.

> I am overwhelmed, crushed and saddened in my identification with your disappointing news regarding Joe,

he said, going overboard in the wonderful way that he had.

> Having shared your happiness about him so recently, I can easily understand what a terrible trauma and disappointment it must be. I can only say good riddance to the jerk if he didn't know how lucky he was to have occupied a spot in your generous and beautiful heart.

Wow! Wasn't it almost worth losing a lover to get a letter like that from a brother? What a lift that gave me! Love!

And, in the same mail, I received another letter that was equally pleasing, from a lady in Leeds, Yorkshire, which is way up by Scotland. I looked in my atlas to see where she was when she sat down at her desk to write to me.

"Dear Ronda Thompson," she wrote,

> I hope you will not mind my writing to you, and there is no need to answer this letter. But I did want to tell you how very much I liked your story, "Love." I hardly ever read magazine stories as usually they are not of high quality, but I had an hour or two's wait and picked up this magazine. Your story touched me very deeply and has haunted me ever since. I loved it.

I always hoped my stories would resonate in someone's mind or heart somewhere out there, and according to this lady in Leeds, so very far away from me in northern California, they did!

I publish only two or three stories a year. They do not win prizes or go into collections, I do not get grants. The stories simply appear and disappear. But I always believed that they touched people, that people were haunted by them, that they laughed at them and cried, and by gum . . .

These two letters made me feel that I was worth something, because what you feel most of all when your lover leaves you is worthless.

If you have given your all in love, if you have not withheld one tiny scrap of yourself, then you can feel a bone-crushing worthlessness when your lover leaves because you gave all and it was not enough and whether your house is small and your dog farts a lot is immaterial because in the end you yourself have been found wanting and your lover has left you for something better.

The letter from the lady in Leeds haunted me as my

story haunted her. It was like my story in tone: clear, odd, sincere, restrained.

As I peeled potatoes for vichyssoise, I answered her in my head:

Lady of Leeds, why did you have an hour or two's wait? That is a very long wait indeed. For what or for whom? Some wait—to drive a lady of your high standards to a magazine! You picked it up, you say. You didn't buy it. So that precludes an airport where the constraint of a two-hour wait is not unusual no matter who you are. Surely no doctor or dentist would have kept you that long. Could you have been in a private home and got it off the coffee table, some home or room strange to you, some way station where you planned a rendezvous and he was delayed?

Dear lady, my story can only have touched you because you too have loved like that. It was written when Joe and I had to meet by subterfuge, when we tried to make a human place out of motel rooms with roses, wine, and laughter. At that time he still was living lovelessly with his wife and we would have to meet in clever places. There was the joy of being together conjoined with the despair of never hoping to get together in a twenty-four-hour-a-day way.

Although the characters were older and didn't look like we do, that was what the story "Love" was about.

We lived and loved like that for a year, until his wife found out and kicked him out. He was glad. He wanted to be the kickee, not the kicker. He couldn't have brought himself to leave her and the children unless she desired him to go. It emerges that the same was true (for he's left me now, Leeds lady) when she desired him to return. By then he'd experienced the smaller house, no piano, less money, guilt perhaps . . .

But he'd experienced love too! Total love! What about that? Doesn't it weigh? Doesn't it count for something?

No, actually not. Put love on the balance and it won't weigh. Not a grain. Love has no quantity of heaviness or mass. How can something so illusory have weight when on the other side of the balance is Property, Substance, Place-In-The-Community, Family, Money.

Joe made the bank his career, not the clarinet, although he loved it so much more. The clarinet was for afterhours. As was I. I tried to persuade him to give up the bank and give his all to his music, his composing, and I still think it would have worked in time. We would have created, for both of us, the life we should have been living.

The potatoes turned from brown to white beneath my paring knife and soon—well, in about an hour—they covered the entire counter. I was leg-weary from standing there. I wondered why I never sat down to peel or to chop, which activities I spent hours at every day.

I washed my hands and went to my writing table to set down some lines of verse that had bubbled up from my hour of peeling and musing.

> *The Avoirdupois Of Love*
> *Love has no quantity of heaviness or mass.*
> *Not a grain.*
> *Not one.*
> *Unless it's unreturned love that does harass*
> *Then it weighs a lot*
> *It weighs a ton*

7 . . .

My plan to shout "I scorn you!" didn't work. My nights were bad. One terrible night I awakened sweating with fear. The hot hairy mass of death was heavy on my chest, its claws were on my neck. I sat bolt upright, screaming. It turned out to be Moby, not death. He'd settled cozily on top of me, purring and kneading.

"Goddamn it, Moby, I won't tolerate this kind of thing

from you. I thought we had an understanding. I refuse to sleep with a cat. If you are even on this bed at all you are to be at the foot of it. What are you doing here anyhow? You're supposed to be out at night, prowling, catching mice, tomcatting around. I'm not so sure I like this new you, all clean and nice. I was proud of your meanness; it set you apart. Not any cat can be as hated as you are in this neighborhood. Are you willing to give up that distinction for a few caresses?"

Blue came over and put his head on the bed for a pat, wanting to get in on the harangue. "It's true, Blue. Once you become a pet, it's awfully hard to become mean and independent again, awfully hard.

"It isn't just missing the security of belonging to someone, it's the desolation of not having someone to love and to care for, to think about and look after, to be needed by. Without Sam, without Joe, I feel I have no anchor, no haven from the stormy sea. I'm bobbing about rudderless, anchorless, winging it, blowing it, confusing my metaphors ..."

One night, when the old people had hobbled off, I couldn't bear to go to bed and since I saw a light on at Mack's place, I decided to go down and ask him if he'd like to run a marathon with me and Maude.

Mack Scher (a shortening of Schereschewsky) lived across the street in a place so small it made my place look like the Djemma el F'na. He got a screwing on his divorce. She got the house, the kid, and most of his salary.

Mack was my age, thirty-five. He had brown eyes, curly auburn hair, a beautiful smile. He looked like James Caan, the movie star, only shorter. He was a terrific person: nice, smart, a good runner, and a good policeman. Sam loved Mack and I did too.

I went down to Mack's—down because his apartment is under the house across the street and approached by a downhill driveway.

He was sitting at his table having some linguine with

clam sauce, and he dished me up a plate. He was in jeans and T-shirt and his uniform was hung neatly in the doorless closet. His holster and gun hung from a hook low on the wall by his bed. This gun, a .38, was his off-duty gun. His on-duty gun, a Smith and Wesson.357, he checked into his locker at the end of duty along with all the other stuff on his belt: radio, cuffs, extra ammo, baton.

"Thanks for returning the handkerchief."

"Not at all," I said, lighting into the linguine, a happy change from soup. "How's business? Have you got a line on the Rapist? I've been reading about him. I read the paper now so I can be abreast of these matters and talk intelligently with you. We'll all be glad when he's collared."

"Oh, we *want* to catch him," Mack assured me in his droll way. "We have that on our list of things to do."

"It's scary to read about him. But I guess it's a good idea to alert the women. They say he's struck four times already right here in town. I don't know why they call him the County Rapist—as if to dignify him with a wider reach."

"Four times that we know about."

"I suppose a lot of women don't report it. Such a horrible experience. And in your own bed! They say that's the worst. If you get raped out on the street, that's bad, but in your own bed it's much worse because if you can't feel safe there, where can you feel safe? God, you'd never want to go to bed at night again."

"Yeah, that's a pretty bad deal all right."

"Tell me more about him, Mack."

"What more can you say than that he's a rapist? He's probably black."

"Women always think rapists and burglars are black because it's the color of evil. I bet he's not. The blacks get blamed for everything. Especially in this white bailiwick."

"We're pretty sure he's black."

"What does he do to the women?"

"Never mind. You'll get yourself all worked up about it."

"The paper said he's incredibly quiet. He comes through the window or door and walks soundlessly to the bed of the sleeping woman."

"Yeah, that's right."

"He has a knife."

Mack nodded.

"Then what?"

"He ties your arms and legs to the bed posts."

"Really? But not many beds have bedposts these days."

Mack looked up, interested. "That's right. We never thought of that. He must check out the beds first. Because every one of these ladies had bedposts."

"I've got bedposts."

Mack poured himself some more wine.

"Then what does he do, Mack?"

"Never mind. That's enough. It's not a good thing to talk about. You'll get nervous. Tell me what you've been up to. Still staking out the Mastersons' house?"

"Only on the full moon." I scowled at him but he just smiled.

I finished the linguine. "Tasty." I carried both our plates to the sink and put on some water for tea. "What I came to ask you was, how would you like to run a marathon with me and Maude? Avenue of the Giants."

"That's not a bad idea," he said, stroking his chin where he wished he still had his beard. The department made him take it off. "Not a bad idea at all."

I knew I had him hooked then because if he began thinking a thing wasn't a bad idea, he ended by thinking it was a damn good idea. It would take him about two weeks before he'd be talking of nothing but the marathon. In the end, however, he probably wouldn't come. That was the way Mack was.

"I don't know though," he said now. "I'll have to think about it."

We talked of other things, then he said, "Avenue of the Giants, eh?" Then we went back to other subjects until he

said, "May seventh. Hmmn." Lots of imaginary beard stroking. "How fast are you going to go?"

"If I come in around four hours I'll be pleased. Twen-
ty-six miles we're talking."

"That's a long way, all right. Not for Maude, though.
She loves those marathons. The harder the better."

Maude had run the Pike's Peak marathon, up seven
thousand feet to the summit of fifteen thousand.

"She's tough," Mack said, "tough as nails. You going up
to the wine country for the fifteen-kilo race on Saturday?"

"Yes. Maude's getting me into the distance. It will be my
longest race so far."

We discussed the different runners we knew, training
schedules, diet, shoes, times. Mack and I could talk for
hours about running, loving every minute of it, fascinated
by the smallest detail, in a way that made a nonrunner
listener suicidal with boredom. I don't know how runners
can find so much to say about a sport that is just putting one
foot in front of another for a given amount of miles, but
they do, and hours after tennis players or footballers have
wrung out the last word on the subject of their sport, runners have just begun to get below the surface to the essence.

"You know, Mack, running really *is* mystical, and in this
talk of shoes and socks and stopwatches, we are searching
for the mystical heart of the matter which, if found, will tell
us what life is. And death. And love too. And truth, why not?
Art."

"What about law and order? Don't forget them."

"I don't think they're in the mystical heart of the matter," I said dryly.

"I don't think I want them to be," said Mack. "It's a
bunch of crap. It's the facts, not the heart, of the matter that
tell us what we need to know about life, death, and truth.
Art, I don't know. That's your territory."

"But cops as well as writers have to use intuition, psychology, imagination, percipience . . ."

"Psychology, yes. Imagination no. You've got to stick

with the facts. A good cop has an analytical mind; the good story writer an intuitive mind. Different."

"It's quite a three-pipe problem."

"What?"

"Quote from Sherlock Holmes." I went to the door. " 'Night, Mack."

"Take it easy."

Mack was right. I did sleep poorly that night, thinking of the Rapist, my nerves on edge. Every sound seemed to me to be identifiable as the Rapist's soundless footsteps. When I did sleep I had bad dreams. Thank goodness for the animals. Blue, although so old, had sharp ears and was a good watchdog. And Moby, sleeping on my bed in defiance of my rule, was a comforting presence who would tear any rapist to shreds who tried to displace him.

8 . . .

Why did Joe leave me?

Three weeks had passed and I was still trying to work it all out. After putting massive amounts of pinto beans on the stove to simmer with pork ribs, onions, and tomatoes, I sat down at my writing table and marked on my calendar the passage of time since Joe had left.

Blue was lying under the table, his snoot on my feet. Moby, on top of the table, gazing grandly out the window, looked magnificent, white as a cloud. Even the ruff of his neck, seldom clean, was spotless. He didn't seem to have one wound. It was as if he had showed his displeasure at having Joe live with me by getting into fights and coming home all vile with gore. I had suspected as much at the time but didn't let it influence me. You can't give a cat that kind of power.

Did Moby have power? Did Blue? How much did their presence bother Joe? Did it matter about Gramps' Night wrecking the soup business, about my being, finally, some kind of success in life? While I hoped to help him create, to compose, did he hope to turn me into a banker? Someone with a big broody house instead of my light, airy habitat of three rooms with hardwood floors, no rugs except for a small moroccan in the writing room, a minimum of furniture—a simple house with a Shaker look and feel to it, spare, monastic, and yet warm too! Always flowers on the table, a fire in the hearth, something bubbling on the stove, the benign presences of a contented cat, a good old dog, often a gaggle of growing boys to serve up soup to in front of the fire (not to mention the gaggle of Gramps' Night)—I didn't ask for more. I had exactly what I wanted—or did have until I relearned the warmth of physical love, the joy of twining myself up Joe's body like a morning glory on a fence. Long sweet kisses to my center until I wanted to burst open like a pomegranate, spilling all my seeds, and his.

Well, life goes on, I thought. But it would go on so much better if I understood. Then I, like Moby, could be healed and magnificent, self-sufficient.

I longed for conclusion.

I wondered how it would be when Joe and I, inevitably, met again for the first time. Would we round a corner and come face to face? Or would it be in some crowded room, our eyes meeting over heads? How would we greet each other, with what words? How control our vibrating voices? Our bodies? Would I freeze or fly? Toward him or away? Should I be vulnerable or proud?

If only I could plan it, call Joe and suggest we try it out, meeting again for the first time, practice seeing each other, practice performing a slight, formal bow of recognition, our hands behind our backs so that they would not autonomically reach out for each other as we tried *not* to remember how it always was when we met before—flinging our arms around each other, Joe lifting me right off my feet and whirling me round and round, kissing me with his lips and tongue all wrapped up amongst mine.

9 ...

*I*t happened two days later. I went to the town library to see a slide show of Joan Erikson's jewelry. Joan and Erik Erikson, white-haired and wrinkled as the sea, were the most beautiful couple in the world. I really went to look at them.

The lights were dimmed, the show began, some late arrivals came. It was Joe and his wife.

My heart blasted against my ribs, an internal explosion, a Hiroshima of the heart. I invoked yogic disciplines and with some careful breathing stilled the reverberations so that my trembling wasn't noticeable for more than three seats away.

All this time the Mastersons stood at the door. The mastadons. Then someone urged them to go to the back of the room where there were still some chairs. This meant passing by me. I sat on a bench against the wall. Joe did not see me there. As he passed by, I did an unaccountable thing. *I* didn't do it. My body did it, with no dictation from the mind. Or my feelings did it. No one is sure where feelings lodge. It could be the pelvic area, or the *hara*, just above the navel, or in the brain, or in the easily galvanized heart. At any rate here's what I did when Joe walked by me in the dark. I reached out with my thumb and forefinger to the back of his thigh and pinched him as hard as I could.

He glanced down of course, saw it was me, passed on. Next, his wife passed by me, chicly dressed (as opposed to me in my jeans) in a pretty flowered skirt which nevertheless didn't disguise or help the fact that she walked just like a duck.

Pinched him I did. As hard as I could!

10 ...

*T*he next day, after making my soup deliveries, I went to San Francisco for my annual pap smear. It was good to see Doc Suppler, who had seen me through two miscarriages, the birth of Sam and my sterilization (for Joe) the year before.

"I want you to tell me if there's any reason I can't train for a marathon," I said.

"No reason at all. That's a wonderful idea. Just be sure you build up your endurance beforehand. Sometimes, when you're older, knees or ankles start bothering you, but that's the only thing that might deter you. I wish *I* had a blood pressure like yours. For sure, go ahead and run marathons. That way you'll probably live forever."

I was glad he had not been cautionary. It perked me up. And my heart lifted even more as I crossed the Golden Gate Bridge, that soaring structure that is like a rainbow because of its beauty that, like a rainbow's, contains surprise and imbues you with a sense of good omen.

As I approached home, I decided to celebrate my good health and spirits by going up on the mountain for a run, something I had not done alone, without Joe, for a year. The mountain was one of the few places we could safely meet, and we used to take every advantage of it.

I changed into running clothes and saw that Gramps had left me some perch he'd caught off the pier. Another good omen. I had only to buy some salt pork, as I already had milk, potatoes, and onions to combine with the fish for a tasty chowder. Tasty and *cheap*.

I picked up the salt pork at the butcher, then drove the Honda up the twisting roads and parked at the Mountain High, a restaurant that served as the hub of many mountain trails. Joe and I had run hundreds of miles together from here. We'd covered all the hiking trails and they had covered us. Running with a man is as intimate as lovemaking.

After our first meeting—the day we met by chance and he ran a little way with me—he wrote a poem for me and left it in my mailbox. It was about our run, gasping instead of talking, seeming to be joined by leaves and sunlight in the summer forest. It was subtle, tender, wooing.

After our first lovemaking, in a room by the sea, on sheets that had wild animals designed on them, I wrote this poem for Joe:

> *My beast makes me sigh so deep.*
> *I never sighed so deep before.*
> *He is teaching me his lore,*
> *Beside, beneath, the ocean roar.*
> *Perhaps we're creatures of the deep—*
> *Profound, subaqueous, a school of two*
> *Who strayed away*
> *From their ocean lair*
> *To a ground of animals*
> *Where*
> *We gasped for water*
> *Instead of air.*

In both poems we gasped. We did a lot of gasping together in the space of our love affair. I think it is an important thing to do.

To gasp is to long with breathless eagerness, to desire, to crave after. Gasp also suggests catching one's breath in a sudden, single, quick, convulsive intake, as from amazement, terror, and the like.

I commenced my run, and I guess it was "as from amazement," the gasp I gave at seeing Ishmael for the first time. I didn't know he was called Ishmael; I learned that later. This day (of many omens) he was a strange man in black running shorts, finishing a run, sweat streaming down his torso, flashing me a big smile as he ran by me. I gasped because he was so sensational-looking.

I ran over a rough trail for about forty-five minutes. I felt a little scared to be running in the woods alone. It was an ordeal, in fact, something I felt I had to do. At first I just kept thinking about when it would be over. "Here I am on the Hukuiku trail so it will be only fifteen minutes until I debouch upon the fire trail. Then, pretty soon I'll be . . ."

But, after a while, the running soothed me, the trees entranced me, the scuffle of a wild creature gave me comfort instead of startle. I fell into an altered state.

Tears began to fall from my eyes but I wasn't sobbing. I let them fall, watering the wind of my passage. I ran very fast. My body felt oiled. My toes had eyes in them. I levitated over rocks and roots.

"Way to go! Good for you!"

These voices brought me back to earth. No, back to civilization, rather, for it was earth I had gone to. It seemed I was passing three women hikers and they were applauding me. I waved and smiled.

Back at the parking lot of the Mountain High, I took a pee in the outdoor privy, exchanged my wet T-shirt for a dry sweat shirt, brushed out my hair, and decided to go into the bar of the restaurant to refresh myself.

The three hiking ladies were going in to lunch. They were deep in conversation but they paused to ask, "How many miles did you run?"

"Oh, six or seven, I guess."

"That's wonderful!"

They went into the restaurant and I stopped at the tiny rustic bar, really rustic, not simulated, being seventy years old. I climbed up on the high wooden stool and ordered a glass of juice. I was the only one there. I could see into the restaurant and beyond the happy heads of eaters-out to the glorious view.

The hiking women were looking over at me from their table. I could tell they were full of admiration for me because I was a mountain runner, because I could come into a bar and sit there by myself and not give a shit. Brave feminists! If they only knew how I missed my man and how he was all I thought about. If they only knew how much I enjoyed the way he treated me so like a woman, a frail woman, with tender concern, gallantry and gentleness, how he . . .

No, I am practicing aloneness today and it isn't good practice to think of him. I must become a different being. I shall develop a new persona. I shall go about, sitting alone in bars, looking unapproachable and sinister. People will point at me and say:

"Yes, that's Ronda Thompson, the writer. Or the soupist. She sits alone in bars, drinking juice. She's done it ever since her lover left. You can't approach her. It's as if she has a magnetic field around her. I knew someone who tried to approach her once when she was sitting like that at a bar and he just crumpled to the floor when he got about a foot away from her. It was the damnedest thing you ever saw. Do you think she looks sinister? No? I don't either. She looks too much like Virginia Woolf to look sinister. Why juice? I don't know. It's always juice she drinks—boysenberry-apple."

"Aren't you Ronda Thompson?" a man asked, approaching me easy as pie.

"Yes."

It was Monsieur Doubin, owner of Le Fromage.

"I was going to call you," he said. "I have a new chef now who desires to do the soups."

"Oh?"

"Yes. Sorry. But it makes more sense, you understand."

"You won't have the variety. Probably onion soup one night, vichyssoise the next. Boring."

"True. But it's more acceptable to our customers. Your soups were often rather... er, off-putting. Chard soup? Pinto bean?" He rolled his eyes as if to say *mon Dieu*, or more likely, *merde alors*.

"My soups are delicious," I said, offended.

"Indeed. This is true. But the customer doesn't know that and often the name, or the look, doesn't encourage them to try and see."

"Pfui."

"Also, recently, my dear, they've been getting a bit thin."

"So's this conversation."

11 . . .

*B*ack down in the town I went into The Splash. Maude was still working. The owner was there looking at Maude, eating his heart out that he couldn't fire her, that she wouldn't smile and, forlornest hope of all, that he couldn't get into her pants.

He sat down with me and chatted for a while. When he left, Maude came over. "Joe was just here for lunch," she said.

"So late?"

"He's been sick. He hasn't been to work in a while. Ronda, he looks awful."

"Well, what did he expect," I muttered. "Of course he's sick." My eyes filled with tears.

Why should I feel sorry for him. Why should he *want* me to feel sorry for him. He'd made his bed.

"He says his whole body hurts."

"I guess he's got the flu."

"No. He knows it's psychosomatic."

"Did he happen to say if he was impotent too? I'd be glad to know if he's impotent."

"He didn't say," Maude answered dryly.

"It doesn't matter. Louise is frigid in any case. Sexually dysfunctional, as they say nowadays. He never talked about her but I gathered that much. I saw her up close for the first time the other day. She's a really big woman. Of course, he's big too. But she must be nearly six feet! I was surprised. Funny to think that I never really saw her up close before. And here am I—five feet four, a hundred and five. It must be like going from a sports car to a Mack truck."

As we talked, Maude efficiently counted her money. "Fifteen dollars in tips today. Not bad. I told the boss I get more tips not smiling because the customers want to make me smile."

"What did he say?"

"He couldn't handle that. Beyond his ken." Maude looked at me searchingly. "Joe's worried about your soup business."

"So am I. I just lost my account at The Cheese."

"Too bad!"

"It's awful. I thought maybe when Joe went back to Louise I might get my private customers back, but no."

"I suppose you're still doing Gramps' Night once a week?"

"No. Twice."

"That's crazy."

"I love them."

"You're nuts." Maude made a *tsk* sound. She was the

only woman I knew that made that old-fashioned *tsk-tsk* sound. It was nice.

She fixed her piercing blue eyes on me. "Joe said he saw you at the library slide show."

"Oh?"

"He said you pinched him."

"Yes, that's right, I did." I felt sheepish.

Maude laughed. She laughed so hard she had to hold her sides. The patrons were astonished. And the owner looked peeved, as if she'd been holding out on him.

"I guess it was a pretty funny thing to do."

She wiped her eyes. "He kept asking me, 'Why did she pinch me? Why? What did she mean by it?' I said maybe you were trying to wake him up from his bad dream. He said there was a lot of anger in that pinch. He said it was a very hard pinch."

"It was difficult to find any flesh on that part of his thigh, with all those muscles. He has the most beautiful legs in the whole world," I mourned. "Poor Joe. I know he is wretched without me. I know he is undergoing the same pain of separation even though he chose it. I should call him. I . . ."

"Don't call him, Miss. You're both much too vulnerable."

"Yes, it would be a terrible setback. I almost have a month under my belt. But Time, the great healer, isn't doing his work. This has been the unhappiest week of all. If I heard his voice it would undo me. And what is there to say? I just have to keep reminding myself that his decision is unalterable. He is unhappy, he misses my love, of course. But he was unhappy when we were together, missing his house and worrying about his family. I guess his happiest time was when he had both. Perhaps he wants to return to that but . . ."

"Don't!"

"I won't. It's unthinkable."

"And don't call him."

"I won't."

When I got home I called him. That is to say I called Wells Fargo and left a message for him to call, knowing he would probably call in sometime today for messages. He called within the hour. We talked for a long time. It was all pure misery. It was all bootless. It was like talking to a man in prison. And for him it must have been like talking to a woman in a madhouse.

"I'm going to run a marathon," I told him.

"I knew you would," he groaned. "I just knew you would decide to do that. Please don't. You'll only hurt yourself."

"I will. I'm going to run it," I said gleefully, glad of his reaction.

"You'll end up looking like . . ." He named a famous older woman runner who looks like a Buchenwald victim.

"That's right, I will! When you next see me you won't know me; I'll be so stringy and sinewy and gaunt. I'll have no bosoms or behind at all. My eyes will be rolling in my head. My . . ."

I elaborated with zest on my ensuing disintegration as a desirable woman. Which was crazy. What did I gain by turning into a scarecrow?

What did I gain by having this stupid conversation? Why not at least say something important?

"How is Louise?"

"All right," he said, very guardedly. "How's the soup business?"

"Well, pretty good. I'd say that Gramps' Night is expanding faster than the business is. I should go about trying to get some orders . . ."

"Why don't you do that?"

"Maybe I'm afraid if I build up the business too much, I'd have no time for my writing. I could give up my running but it's such a pleasure to me. It makes me feel so good—

especially now—and it's only an hour out of the day, not counting the subsequent lone-juicing . . ."

"The what?"

"Actually, I'm thinking of getting the old people out running. It will get their minds off their diseases. God, that's all they talk about! I've got to expand their horizons."

"Watch out or they'll be talking about running injuries instead. Sore hamstrings instead of lung cancer."

"I'll be careful to start them out very slowly. A half-mile at the track, just walking. They . . ."

"I want to know about *you*, Ronda. Tell me, please, a little about yourself."

"I'm fine. I'm learning to be . . . alone." That's what I told Joe, that I was fine, and that I was learning to be alone. I didn't say:

I'm scared.

I'm broke.

My soups are getting thinner.

My heart is an open wound.

"And you?" I asked blithely. "What is your life like now?"

"It's . . . It's fine."

When I hung up, I sat by the phone sobbing. After a while the phone rang and it was Sam, calling from U.C. San Diego. I'd written him about Joe.

"Hi, Mom."

"Sam! How are you, sweetheart?"

"Fine, how are you."

"I'm okay. I'm pretty good."

"Hey, look. When are you going to run this marathon?"

"In May. The seventh. I've got four months to train up."

"Well, I think I'll run it with you, okay?"

"You will? Really! Oh, Sam, that's wonderful!"

"Not *with* you exactly. I'll be miles ahead actually. You'll have to eat my dust."

"Ho ho! That's what you think. You watch me. You'll be

running along, feeling all cocky and all of a sudden you'll hear this pit-pat, pit-pat behind you and you'll look back to see who it is and there, pulling up abreast of you, moving ahead of you, will be . . ."

"Bill Rodgers."

I laughed. It was so good to laugh. God, it was good to talk to Sam and to laugh. What a boy. What a kid. What a lucky mother I was. Imagine him calling to say he'd run the marathon with me. I thought:

When your lover leaves and you get a loving letter from your brother and your cat pulls himself together and your best friend and your own son say they'll run a marathon with you, then is that such a bad thing, to have your lover leave, when such loving things come of it? Is it? Is it?

"Is old Mack going to run it?" Sam asked.

"He's thinking about it."

We both laughed, knowing how Mack was.

"How's Ronda's Soup Service?"

"Terrific."

"Okay, well, 'bye."

"Thanks for calling. I love you."

12 . . .

A terribly embarrassing thing happened a few days later, at dusk. Having come off the mountain from an eight-mile run, I was reentering the town on the street that comes down from the park and library. I saw Joe drive up in his adorable car, an old Alfa Romeo that we both just loved. He parked, got out, and was immediately joined by his wife and two friends, who greeted him exuberantly. They walked along together, talking and laughing, and turned into Consuelo's, a favorite restaurant of Joe's.

I felt stricken. It seemed to me that life went gaily on apace for Joe while I continued to suffer.

While I staggered around with my entrails hanging out, bleeding and weeping, he went into restaurants, talking and laughing.

I came abreast of the Alfa. Without thinking, I squatted down and let the air out of the two curb tires. I just did it for no reason, a stupid, meaningless gesture.

At that moment, unbeknownst to me, Mack emerged from an apartment house by which the Alfa was parked. He was in uniform. Naturally he was curious to investigate this squatting figure and, getting closer, to identify the unmistakable hissing sound of escaping air from one tire and the unmistakable blubbered-down look of already-escaped air from the other tire.

"Hey, Ronda! What's going on here?"

I stood up. The blood rushed to my face. I wrung my hands.

"What did you do that for?"

"I . . . I don't know," I stammered. "I honestly don't know. I just . . . did it."

Your Body Grieves

1 . . .

Mack let me go, of course. After all, we're best friends. But he came over to my house later and pointed out to me: "That's a misdemeanor, Ronda. Malicious mischief. Six months in jail or a five-hundred-dollar fine. Or both." He actually pointed his finger at me as he talked, jabbing the air. "I just thought you should know that for the future. I just came by to let you know that."

"Malicious? Me, Mack?" I felt wounded.

"Yeah, you. That's *twice* now. What about the time you were up at his house?"

"Nothing about it."

"What did you do while you were up there?"

"Nothing. I just looked at the house. I'm interested in architecture."

"Well cut it out. Just forget the guy, will you? Forget him and get on with your life and keep out of mischief."

"Okay." I hung my head, humbled.

He slammed out of the house. He was pretty pissed off at me.

What about the pinch, I wondered. Was that malicious mischief too? A five-hundred-dollar fine or a half-year in jail? Good thing Mack doesn't know about the pinch, I thought, or else he could say it was *thrice* now.

He's right. I'm going to forget the guy.

But then a few days later I received in the mail an unexpected boon. It was a money order for fifteen hundred dollars. A covering letter disclosed that it was a prize for my short story, "Love," from an anonymous donor who aimed to encourage the art of short fiction in America.

I was so pleased and excited that I thought only of telling someone the news, someone being Joe.

My heart was beating so fast that the blood was coursing through my body like a riptide. I completely lost track of time, of space, didn't know where I was in either of them, seemed actually to forget that Joe had left me, was transported back to the time of our being together, or before that, or beyond it to no-time.

I was in an unaccountable state when I called Joe.

As it was early morning, I called him at his home, which I had never done before.

A woman answered the phone—Louise, of course. Temerariously I said, "This is Ronda Thompson. May I speak to Joe, please? It's important."

So full of power and exhilaration was I, so crazed with joy and excitement, that I simply demanded that Louise put her husband on the phone to his ex-mistress.

Well, we have rights too, don't we? Some rights? Ex-mistresses are human beings too. Not to wives, maybe. Maybe not even to husbands. But *we* know we're human beings.

Presently his voice came carefully through the instrument. "Hello?"

"Joe! Guess what? I've wonderful, wonderful news. I've just won fifteen hundred smackers for my love story. An anonymous prize from a fiction lover. Imagine! Imagine fiction lovers even having money to give away! I was thinking we could use the money to enlarge the living room and then bring down your piano and . . ."

"But, Ronda . . ."

"A music room at last! You can compose. We can begin our musical comedy!"

"Ronda, I . . ."

"Oh, darling, it's hard for you to talk, isn't it. I'm sorry. I wasn't thinking. I just had to call you right away to tell you the grand news. But wait a minute, I'm all confused. I forgot you'd left me. How weird. And how embarrassing. I actually forgot for a minute, in all the excitement, that you'd gone back to Louise. It's not that I was trying to woo you back with the money. Please don't think . . . Joe?"

"I think I'd better come over and see you. I'll come by right away and we'll talk."

I hung up the phone, tore into the bathroom, quickly showered, brushed my hair, laid on the Christian Dior cologne, put on my purple pants, which are strictly for high-energy occasions, and the Ralph Lauren shirt Joe gave me for my birthday, white with thin blue stripes.

I was trembling with excitement. He's coming back to me, I thought. He's coming home. Blue, sensing my inner commotion, began to bark and run around in circles. I took some minutes to calm him and summoned some serenity for myself while I was at it.

By then the time had passed that it would take Joe to come so I went out to greet him—but he came not.

I waited by the picket fence, looking down the lane in the direction by which he would arrive. No Joe.

I returned to the house. I paced. I went again to the fence but felt afraid to leave the phone. I returned to the house. I sat by the phone in my writing room. I sat and gradually I knew he would not come.

What had happened? What was happening? What did happen when I called?

I cast my imagination through the valley and up the hill into his house. This is what I saw:

Joe had been in the bathroom shaving when I made

my call to him. He was shaving with the razor I had given him long ago when we were beginning lovers: "So you'll think of me every morning." He was shaving and thinking of me and missing me excruciatingly. Living with me, he'd grown accustomed to joy. Now the day stretched relentlessly ahead of him without any highlight to enhance it.

He shaved, pulling his chin skin this way and that.

The phone rang. He knew with a certainty that it would be me because we are still connected. He knew it would be me even though I'd never called him at his house before.

Soon he saw his wife's face behind him in the mirror. Her face looked frozen; her lips were set in a funny way.

"Ronda Thompson is on the phone," she said, through frozen, twisted lips.

He saw she was afraid and he felt sorry. She followed him to the phone and stood oppressively near him while he talked. He turned his back to her but her presence was so palpable she could have been leaning on him with all her might, with all her considerable weight. "I'll come by right away and we'll talk," he said to me and then he replaced the receiver. He turned. Now the frozen face was hot with blood. The blood was in her face and the eyes bulged. He spoke casually, hoping to avert a scene, hoping to still the torrent of abuse he knew was building up in her. "Something has happened to upset Ronda," he said very casually. "I'll just stop by on my way to work."

"If you go to her now, don't ever come back."

His heart leaped like a child's. Did she mean it? Nothing could make him happier. He would go at once. And never return again. He felt like a condemned man granted a last-minute reprieve. But did she *mean* it? In a second she might say something completely opposite. He must seize the moment and fly. All the reasons for leaving Ronda were as nothing now, chaff.

"I mean it," she said. "Why should you come at her summons? Who cares if she's 'upset'? If you go to her, parking your car outside her house for all the world to see, never come back here. You've flaunted this affair before the entire town, shaming me. I took you back. I know you well and knew you were ripe to return to me. I forgave the suffering you'd inflicted on me, put aside all pride. Since your return, I've gone out of my way to try to make a new beginning. If you go . . ."

Joe, remembering the phone conversation, realized that Ronda somehow connected his leaving her with his not being able to have his piano. But that had never crossed his mind! What a terrible thing for her to think.

Why *had* he left her then? His mind was a blank. He couldn't imagine why. Something to do with Louise . . .

"I won't go to Ronda," he said.

He couldn't bear to go through it all again. He hadn't the strength. If only Louise would just be quiet . . .

The thing was, he thought, Louise needed him, Ronda really didn't. Ronda was—he searched for a word, found it, believed it—*valiant.*

Tears rushed to his eyes and his throat convulsed. He turned away from Louise. "I'll just call Ronda and tell her I won't be coming. You see, something unexpected happened and she couldn't deal with it. That's why she called. But she'll be all right. She'll be all right."

He reached for the phone . . .

2 . . .

*A*nd just as my imagination had carried the scene to this point, sure enough, the phone, my phone, rang. In my mind Joe was reaching for the phone and in my writing room it rang. Uncanny? No. I was not surprised. These things don't surprise me. We are so deeply connected, Joe and I.

So I reached for the phone. But it was not Joe. No, it was not Joe at all. It was Doctor Suppler on the wire.

It was Doc Suppler and he said, "Your pap smear didn't test out normal, Ronda. I think you'd better come in to see me today. I'll put my nurse on the line and you can set up an appointment."

"Wait! Tell me more! Not normal? Not normal in what way? What does it mean?"

He lapsed into medical lingo that I couldn't understand. By not comprehending I was able to try to turn his gobbledegook into a positive statement. "Well, that sounds normal to me," I said. "I mean, isn't that a little bit normal?"

"You come on in and we'll talk about it. I want to get another pap smear which I'll send to a different lab and I want to get some tissue for a biopsy. Then we'll see. Hold on now."

I set up the appointment for three o'clock, hung up the phone and sat there trembling. Now my imagination really raced. The trip across the valley to Joe's house was as nothing compared to this journey; child's play.

In a matter of seconds I traveled the whole route of health, disease, operation, pain, disintegration, death. Then I backtracked to before the operation to write my will and arrange for Sam. Should I sell the house and set up a trust? When should Sam be told? If ever. Should I tell any of my friends? Maude? Joe?

Oh my God, Joe!

My mind returned again to the writing room. Joe still might walk into my house at any moment. He mustn't come back to me now. You don't ask your lover back if you've got a mortal disease. Despite the scene I had imagined, he could be stepping in here right now. He said he'd be *right* over. How long ago was that? Should I call? What if I get Louise again? Never mind. I'd better call. But what will I say?

I picked up the receiver and dialed, hoping some words would come to me. He answered. "Hello?"

"Joe? You're still there? That's good. I . . . I've got myself together now. I didn't know what I was saying earlier. I didn't mean to put you on the spot like that. Of course I don't expect you back because of this . . . development. I was thrown off center. I don't seem to be able to think before I act these days."

Oh Joe, I wanted to cry. Help me! I'm *not* valiant. I'm scared to death. Hold me! I need you.

"Joe, are you there?"

"Yes, I'm here. I won't come by, then, Ronda, but I'm very glad about the prize. I'm proud of you. It's a fine story. Please use the money to help your business, maybe hire someone to help you with the gardening, or the washing up. Take *care* of yourself. Please?"

"Care? Oh yes. Thank you. Well, good-bye . . ."

"Good-bye, Ronda."

I hung up the phone. He was still there, at his house, and he wasn't coming back, he was coming *by*. But he hadn't even come by. He was still there, still there, telling Louise he would not ever see me again.

I'm so alone. Boy, am I ever alone.

At my writing-room window four incredible pink roses pressed against the glass as if trying to see in. Four rogue roses blooming and peering. The last roses of summer in January, trying to give me heart.

3 . . .

*T*hat night the County Rapist struck again. For the first time in two months. This time it was in my neighborhood.

For a week the town talked of nothing else, but for once I was uninterested. I was too busy trembling beneath the sword. I went in for my biopsy on the Friday. The lab couldn't go to work on it until Monday. So I wouldn't hear until the following Wednesday or Thursday. In the meantime I languished, thinking, oh, for some precognitive powers now when I need them!

My fate was never off my mind, which kept churning around all the possibilities, having no sense at all of which way it would go. It seemed inconceivable to me that I could be diseased, and yet there was that accursed test that said I probably was. There was Doc Suppler saying, "I don't think they'll find anything, Ronda," but there was also the moment, engraved on my mind, that he peered inside me for the biopsy and declared, "I see a place I'd better get some tissue from."

Running, I felt so strong and fleet, I knew that I was well.

But when I lay down at night I felt my body crumbling away into a million pieces and I knew I was rapidly diminishing in health and life and would probably be dead by morning.

I kept writing my will in my head at night.

I kept thinking about "the place" Doc Suppler saw, trying to envision it, beautify it.

If the tissue from the biopsy proved malignant, I would go at once to have my cervix removed and my uterus.

Then my kidney, my lungs, my heart, my bowels, and my bosoms.

Strangely, what all my churning thoughts came back to

time and time again was: whom did I want to drive me to the
hospital? Sam? Maude? Mack?

I didn't tell anyone. Except Blue. I talked a lot about it
to Blue. Not Moby, though. Cats don't understand that sort
of thing. Cats don't care. Blue thumped his tail in a slow
sympathetic rhythm as I told him of my woe.

But, of course, Blue couldn't drive me to the hospital.

I didn't see Maude. I ran once with Mack, to the next
town and back. When we parted he looked at me and asked,
"Are you all right?"

I guess my face reflected my dread disturbance. "Sure,
I'm fine."

"Too bad about the Rapist striking so near."

"I can handle that." The Big C made even rape insignif-
icant. "After all, Mack, a rapist is only a person."

Mack looked puzzled. "What? You mean as opposed to
an act of nature?"

"Yes, or a war, or a disease. But for the amount of fear
he generates—among women—you'd think he was something supernatural."

"That's right."

"Maybe the reason rapists are so successful is that they
have so much fear going for them." Maybe that's why cancer
is too, I thought.

Back in the house, shedding my wet running clothes, I
vowed to contend with it. If I am malignant, I swore, I will
lick it. I will fight it to the death and win. I will show the
world a struggle that will make Laocoön's look limp-wristed.
Or no! Better, maybe, to embrace it rather than fight it.
Embrace it in the spirit of St. Francis.

I got my copy of Chesterton's *St. Francis* to find those
most moving lines spoken by St. Francis before his operation.

He was going blind. The remedy in those days was
worse than the disease. What they did was cauterize the eye
without anesthetic. They put an iron in a furnace until it was
red hot, then laid it on his living eyeball, intending to burn

the blindness away. As they took the glowing red brand from the furnace, Francis rose to his feet. He made a lovely, almost casual gesture with his hands and addressed the hot iron in this way: "Brother Fire, God made you beautiful and strong and useful; I pray you be courteous with me."

Oh to have such courage, such quietude of soul, such . . . gentleness.

4 . . .

I took a group of old people to the track the afternoon before Gramps' Night. I'd spent some of the prize money buying them good running shoes, and I gave them all the big sell on how this running was going to help their hearts, arteries, lungs, and arthritic limbs. I told them it would make them feel more sexy too.

Only about ten of them agreed to give it a try. They were all pretty skeptical. The rest of them came to observe and to heckle.

The gorgeous stranger in the black running shorts whom I'd seen on the mountain and whom I later came to know as Ishmael was doing intervals on the track—55-second 440s, it looked like to me. Not too shabby.

We gave him the inside lane and navigated ourselves around the outside lanes, being quite a contrast to his fleet, mercurial youth.

It was so moving to me to see those old bodies trying to run. It had been fifty or sixty years for some of them since, as children, they had run hither and yon just as easily as breathing, not giving it a thought. I believe the body was made to run for all its life, made to and wants to, but the burden of work, childbearing and rearing slows our steps, the availability of wheels stops them entirely, and we appease our bodies' disappointment with eating and drinking and drugging.

The old people stepped out!

True to my predictions, they talked about running all during dinner, drowning out the chronic complainers, but it was sort of a shame because by then I was wanting to talk about *my* cancer.

I needed to talk to someone besides Blue.

So the next night I went to Maude's house, sat down in her ratty old wing chair until she emerged from the kitchen. She took one look at me and asked, "What's wrong?" Whereupon I burst into tears and said I might have cancer.

I thought I was strong but it only took a sympathetic look from Maude to make me crack. But the strain had been awful. It had been a horrible, horrible five days. Why shouldn't I cry? It felt good to cry and to talk. Tail-thumping as a response was helpful and comforting as far as it went, but it was good to spend an hour with Maude, my friend of so many years, in her nice house that was warm, clean, cozy, full of stuffed chairs and Turkish carpets— where little children came and went in friendly, unobtrusive ways, and from a bedroom practice session came the heart-breaking sound of a flute.

Maybe I wished she'd build a fire more often but heck, I could go to my house for that. It's hard for a woman on her own to get wood—along with everything else. And Maude would be the first to point out that although, granted, I always had a fire, the studio couch on which one was constrained to sit in order to enjoy the fire was the most uncomfortable piece of furniture in the world. The only alternative was the floor which, she said, although softer, was colder.

Maude gave me a cup of tea with a shot of rum in it, my first booze ever.

I talked and talked. I moaned and whined, blubbering into my tea. "It's unfair. What have I done to deserve this? I've been a good mother to Sam. In my writing I have an affirmative vision, good values. I celebrate life, rarely have said a word against it. I behave well all in all, a little mischievous from time to time. It's true I've been an adulteress. Have I? Or is just the married person the adulterer? In any case, that was bad, I know. I could be being punished for that."

"Oh for Christ's sake," said Maude. "You are not being punished just because you loved some guy."

"But is it really adultery if the man isn't sleeping with his wife?" I asked, feeling more interested now in the semantics of the word than in my moral state. "Not sharing her bed at all? Because he didn't, I'm sure. Granted they were legally married at the time, but that's just paperwork. A real marriage is when you're physically joined. When you are one organism taking sustenance from each other through a daily flesh connection."

"Daily?" Maude was impressed.

"Well, pretty daily."

"Hmpff." Maude often hmpffed as well as tskked.

"You should find another lover," she said. "Enough time has gone by—a couple of months."

"It took me three years after Alan died. I'm a long mourner."

"More tea?"

"No. I should go," I said, not budging. "It was good tea, though. I feel better. I'm going to be all right. I know I am. And if I'm not, if I do have cancer, I'll . . ." I didn't want to tell her I'd embrace it and have to go into the whole St. Francis explanation, so I said the conventional, "I'll lick it."

"That's the spirit." She went to the kitchen, came back, handed me another tea with rum in it.

I drank and sighed. I decided to tell Maude about calling Joe the morning I'd gotten my prize money. I told her about the two phone conversations and what I'd imagined in between. It was a long story. I believe I had another tea with rum in it. Maybe I didn't tell the story right. It went on and on. How could it have been so long? I fixed poor Maude with a glittering eye, compelling her to hear me out. I weaved a tale of immense complexity out of wholly imaginary strands. I created the character of Louise—this woman I'd never said boo to, whom I'd seen only once up close and that in a darkened library room as she walked by me in a flowered skirt. I described her with all the authority of one who has ghosted her autobiography. It seemed to me that the darker the shadow I could thrust Louise into, the kindlier the light I could shed on Joe.

I gradually transformed her from the chic and elegant mayoress of the town to a gibbering maniac, a Jekyll-and-Hyde personality.

Finally able to get a word in, Maude said (and I'm sure only because her tongue, too, was rum-loosened), "Joe sent you that prize money."

It took my breath away. "What?" I gasped.

She began to laugh. "It's so funny. He sent you that money because he was so worried about your finances and your first thought was to spend it on him."

"Joe was worried?"

"Of course he was—is. So am I. The Splash is your only customer left. Joe knows that and he knows you've been boycotted by the smart set. I didn't tell him, Ronda. He makes it his business to know. He wanted to give you some money you'd accept. I suggested the prize idea."

"Guilt money."

"No, concern money. Use it to put in your spring garden, why don't you? And to tide you over until your business picks up."

"Or to pay for my hospital bill," I said gloomily.

I slurped air out of my empty cup and rose to go. Maude said she would drive me home but I said no, a little walk would do me good. There was a small altercation about it but I got my way and presently I found myself out on the road. It was a fine night, preposterously starry. I tried that old trick of looking up at the firmament so as to feel diminished so as to make my human problems seem laughable. Of what importance was I, after all, in the scheme of the cosmos?

It didn't work. I felt tremendously important. I can't die yet, I thought. I want to love again. I want to see the great wall of China and reread Chekhov's short stories. I want to write one short story as well as Chekhov did. Just one. Before I die. I want to see Sam well on his way in life, with good love and good work. Love and work, eh Freud? You understood something—not much, but something.

Ah, the universe isn't all that big. It's probably confounded to see me looking up at it. It probably wonders what I mean and how I got here and where I end. How did she begin, the universe asks, and where will she end, or is she simply returning in on herself?

The universe and I are confounded by each other, Entropy. What about entropy, huh? Or muscular dystrophy? What about calligraphy? Omar said:

> *The Moving Finger writes: and, having writ*
> *Moves on: nor all thy Piety nor Wit*
> *Shall lure it back to cancel half a Line*
> *Nor all thy tears wash out a Word of it.*

Piety, wit, and tears. That's me in a nushtell—nutshell. Why would I say nushtell? Yes, the Cosmos' Great Calligraphy In The Sky keeps writing out my life but I do too. I, too, am a writer, only unlike the universe, I have the power to erase. Yes sir! Correcto-tape.

I found I had wandered into someone's yard.

It was embarrassing. But they were understanding. I explained that I had lost my way. We laughed about it a lot. Or I did.

"Better than being in a mushtell," I said. "I mean . . . Well, never mind." Nutshell is what I really meant to say, I assured myself. I could say nutshell if I really wanted to.

Soon—in no time at all it seemed—I was back in my own neighborhood and Blue was greeting me in an aban-

donment of joy. He escorted me triumphantly down the
lane. The *Marseillaise* came to mind and to my voice. Someone shouted "Shut up!" We had some trouble with the gate
latch, a little difficulty with the door handle, but morning
found me safely tucked into the writing-room rug.

I'd written this poem:

> *In A Nutshell*
> *There isn't mushtell*
> *Strike the ancient bell*
> *A long lugubrious knell*
> *For me, not thee, it tolls*
> *While running on the hills*
> *(The bare knolls)*
> *I toll ya all I knoll*
> *There wasn't mushtell*
> *Here it is—in a nutshell*
> *Death hits a homer when life fouls*
> *Never send to knoll*
> *For whom the bell growls*

5 ...

*I*t was only a scare. The biopsy was benign and
Doc Suppler said we'd just watch it and have a
pap test more frequently.

My cervix was only expressing its grief at losing Joe.
Why not? Grief is all in the body. One sighs and cries and
generally languishes. The heart aches. How natural for
one's sex to express itself too, by showing its loneliness,
unhappiness, and dis-ease.

Joe chanced to call me the morning I was awaiting the
definitive call from Doc Suppler. I told him I couldn't talk to

him just then because I was waiting to hear the biopsy result. I said I felt confident that all would be well and that I would let him know.

As soon as I got the good word, therefore, I left a message for Joe and immediately he wrote this letter to me:

> I want to say that I think you are the most wonderful, the most valuable person on the planet at present. You are so full of life and love and good intentions for all creatures that it is breathtaking. You must take care of yourself physically and psychically, and let that glow of yours reach to the ends of the universe. I've shown it poorly but I want to say I've never loved anyone as I've loved and do love you. I can't imagine I ever will. I want good things to happen for you. You deserve it in every way. Please run for fun. Breathe, glow, live, thrive, prevail. I truly care for you.

Notice he said breathe, not gasp. He didn't want me to desire, crave after, or be amazed by, another man. But how was I to glow, thrive, and prevail without love? How was I to maintain my fullness of life, love, and good intentions without sex, which gave me much of that glow he wished to reach to the ends of the universe?

Running made me glow, of course, a glow of health, of coursing blood and all. Run for fun, Joe said. He didn't want me training for a marathon. But I was.

At least I told people I was. I still had not gotten my mileage up. It's hard to get your mileage up when you think you are dying of cancer. So I lost that week and then it rained day and night for thirty days. The mountain sang with running waters. There were springs, creeks, and falls that my old-timers said had not revealed themselves for years.

I rented a tent for Gramps' Night with what I still called

the prize money. We ran at the track regardless of rain, and some of my pals were up to a mile of nonstop running.

Otherwise, Moby, Blue, and I huddled indoors—all of us feeling a bit frail and dependent on each other.

But, imperceptibly, the days were getting longer. Soon the acacias would be in bloom and clouds of yellow would dominate the vistas.

"Let us take tentative steps out into the world as spring comes," I said to Moby and Blue. "Let us find lovers. Even you, Blue, old as you are, could find a pretty bitch to love. I'll get you groomed, buy you a nice new collar. What do you say? *I'm* game. I'll find a lover if you guys will. It's been three long, lonely months now. I want a man and I think I know just what sort of a man. Nothing fancy. Just someone young and beautiful who's a fast runner with a big smile and black running shorts . . .

Running

1 ...

*T*he first real meeting between me and the man in the black running shorts was in Paradise Produce, where I was bagging some small tangerines when he walked in the door. We nodded and smiled slightly at each other as two people do who are not unfamiliar to each other.

But he was so good-looking that, after nodding, I turned shyly away and immersed myself in the selection of salad greens. Physical beauty in people affects me that way; instead of staring I turn away, realizing that if I allowed myself to look, I would become lost in looking and make that person uncomfortable. I feel I am invading their privacy to look at them, taking the gift of their beauty without asking or without it being offered, so I turn away for fear of offending them.

But while my produce was being checked out and bagged, he came up to me in a friendly, open way, saying, "Aren't you a runner? Haven't I seen you at races?"

"Well no, not at races. I just run . . .around."

"At the track, that's where. You're the girl with the pack of old runners."

"Yes. They're getting very strong, you know. They're up to a mile, some of them. It's amazing, the regenerative powers even among ancients."

"My name is Ishmael Scott," he smiled, "but you can call me Joe; everyone does."

"I'll call you Ishmael. Hmmn, that's a good first line for a novel." We laughed. "I have a cat named Moby," I added.

"White, I bet."

Then, as runners will, we launched off into an exuberant conversation about running and routes to run—always on the search for new ones—until he asked, "Why don't you ever come on the Sunday mountain runs?"

"That's out of my league. You guys are tough."

"No, we wait. We wait for you to catch up. Come on up and join us this Sunday."

"Well, I'll see," I said vaguely. I told him I would run my first marathon in May and he said he'd never run one, liked the shorter distances, particularly loved the mile.

"Doc Sheehan says, 'The mile is a lonely and painful and beautiful place. And it must be run as the poetess wrote of love, to the depth and breadth and height my soul can reach.' "

"Yes," Ishmael nodded. "Sheehan understands." He shot me an interested look as if to say that I, too, obviously understood.

I backed off. "Although Mrs. Browning certainly wouldn't have. She didn't have the mile in mind at all. Well, nice talking with you. 'Bye."

"Wait. What's *your* name?"

"Ronda Thompson."

"I'll see you Sunday, Ronda."

"Maybe."

2 . . .

I went to the Sunday mountain run, dragging along Mack and Maude for fortification. The valley was all in fog but as we drove up the mountain, we surfaced above it. The town became lost beneath a cloud of white and at the Mountain High parking lot it was cool but clear. Runners gathered until we numbered fifteen.

There was only one other woman. She had thick red hair, loose to her waist, and exquisitely applied eye makeup. Her smooth pale skin looked like it never saw the light of day or knew any kind of weather. Small and delicately built from the waist up, only her powerful legs hinted at the fact that she was the toughest and fastest mountain-running woman in the county if not the whole world. Among the men I recognized a USA record holder for twenty miles and a world-class marathoner who had brought a Kenyan stee-plechaser. The situation looked grave for me and Mack and Maude.

Ishmael arrived and greeted us pleasantly. When we began the run, he took off with the USA record holder. We started running up. Up to the top of the mountain—about four miles of unrelieved up. The runners of varying abilities strung out in a line, but it was only a matter of seconds before we were *way* behind. However, true to Ishmael's word, they were waiting for us at the top.

"See," I said to Mack and Maude, trying to give us heart, "they're waiting for us at the top, just like Ishmael said."

"And see," said Maude, as soon as we got there, "they'll start off again now that we're here—so who gets to catch their breath? Not us. And who needs to catch their breath? Not them."

"But look! We'll have to go down now. There's no place

to go from this mountaintop but down. Isn't that wonderful?"

"That's great," said Mack. "But they're going down the other side, the north side. Do you know what that means?"

"It means we'll have to run up again," said Maude.

"In order to run back down the south side," said Mack.

"Oh." Indeed, they were all starting off again, heading north.

"See ya," said Mack, turning back the way we'd come.

"But Mack!"

"See ya," said Maude, following him.

"But Maude . . ."

"They're too fast. It's no fun. Come back with us."

I wavered but decided to stick with the group.

"Traitors!" I shouted after them.

Then I joined the runners who, whooping like Indians, ran and leaped and darted and flew down the narrow, winding, rocky path. Here I could stay with them quite well. The group energy and joy gave wings to my feet: the whooping, the breathing, the pounding of feet, the laughter, the sense of being one of a tribe off on a long hunt, in touch with the earth and sky, was exhilarating.

Too soon, alas, it was all over with the downward portion, on with the up, and these runners ran upward with the same élan as downward. It was all one to them. I got a stomach cramp and lagged more and more behind. I begged them to go on without me, but that was against their credo. One was always waiting for me. Later, hearing the sounds of traffic, I said I would go to the road and hitchhike back, but then Ishmael himself was beside me, urging me on. We ran together but I felt I was spoiling his run and said, "Really, I know this trail like I know my own front yard. Please go on and don't wait for me. I know my way perfectly."

He went on.

I ran until I cramped up, walked until I uncramped and, running and walking in this way, gradually made my way back to the car. As I wobbled down the last steep trail, Ishmael was coming up. "I was going to come searching for you. I'm sorry, Ronda. I never would have asked you to come had I known we would do a fourteen-miler this morning. This was one of our toughest runs."

"Oh really?" I said bitterly. "I thought this was your beginner's run."

All the last lone part of the way I had been sustained by the thought of the Mountain High being at the end of my journey. There I could go and be the sinister lone juice drinker again while recovering from this ordeal.

But no. This was not allowed me. Their custom was to go to a coffee shop down in the town and have huge country breakfasts.

We repaired there and I watched them eat, unable to do so myself—my stomach still in a spasm, and my legs still trembling from their recent battles with gravity. I watched Ishmael put down enough ham and eggs and potatoes for three men and sipped resentfully at my coffee.

When we parted company, it did not seem important or even sensible ever to meet again.

But the days passed and as I prepared my vegetable garden for spring planting—weeding, fertilizing, turning the soil—I found he was often on my mind. I remembered nice things about him, nice ways of being he had. I recalled a gentle way he had of taking my arm, a gentle, gallant way of taking me by the elbow and guiding me back onto the trail when I was trying to get away, trying to escape to the highway and hitchhike. I saw in my mind's eye how he looked being a one-man search party coming to find me. He had stripped off his running shirt, revealing long, broad, sloping shoulders, clear-sculpted pectorals and biceps. Most runners have no upper-body strength, distance runners particularly, but Ishmael liked the mile. He must have worked with weights, too, so as to engage his whole body in that race, to bring his whole being to that lonely, painful, beautiful place—the mile.

So one sunny day, all redolent with spring, after I had put in three hours of writing and two of souping, I decided to dedicate one and a half to finding Ishmael. I didn't know where in town he lived and we had no mutual friends from whom I could learn how to get in touch with him, so I simply had to go to town and hope to run into the fellow.

I walked to town to find him. I walked jauntily toward town, facing traffic, in case he was in a car. I thought about my writing. In the last month I'd got back to a good writing schedule. I was writing a new short story called "The Camel Lady by Moonlight." I'd recently sold a story in England for eighty pounds and one in Singapore for eight-five dollars. I'd got word that a story was a finalist for a book of drinking stories the National Council on Alcoholism was publishing. I was feeling good about my writing.

In town, I perambulated the square, browsed through the bus depot, walked on to the library. No Ishmael to be seen.

At the library I went to the encyclopedias to take notes on camels. Camels, I learned, are stupid, recalcitrant, obnoxious, untrustworthy, and openly vicious.

Then I walked back toward town, deep in thoughts of camels. Such patient, sweet, soft-eyed, smiling faces they had. All an illusion. The long lashes were for keeping out the dust, and the muscular nostrils, geared for closing against the dust, caused the belying twist to the lips that gave all the seeming of a smile.

I sauntered along, thinking about camels, trying to open and close my nostrils at will, but not forgetting about my search for Ishmael. Now, rather than consciously looking for him, I was simply making myself visible for his finding of me. I put the ball in his court, so to speak, so I could address myself to camel ruminations, but I still exercised all the power of my intentionality.

I drew abreast of The Splash and naturally stopped in to say hello to Maude. Thirty seconds later Ishmael stepped through the same door. I turned and there he was.

I think now that this might have been the worst thing that could have happened. It seemed so wonderful to me, so incredible, so astonishing that what was, after all, only a chance meeting in a small town assumed mythic proportions. It seemed that destiny was at work, that some higher power was manifesting itself here so that, all reason destroyed, I fell instantly in love.

Discerning Maude, assessing the situation at once, suggested that Ishmael and I sit down together and have lunch.

We ordered lunch and it emerged that he was a juicer too. He was nice. I liked our lunch. We had a good, learning-about-each-other talk. He seemed honest and open about himself. He had been raised in a rich Catholic family, gone to good schools, graduated from college and then—begun his descent into the mire. He became an apostate, raised hell, spent a fortune, got disowned by his family. Now at twenty-nine he was trying to put his life back together. He had foresworn drugs, liquor, gambling, and women and was working as a carpenter, running, thinking, writing lyrics for songs.

His life seemed familiar to me. Why was that? Why was it ringing bells?

Ah ha! St. Francis! It exactly paralleled Francis's life. Even to the songwriting. St. Francis was never a runner. But what a walker! He traversed whole countries on his feet.

I looked at Ishmael narrowly, wondering if he thought he was St. Francis. We would make one hell of a couple if we both thought we were St. Francis.

"What about you?" he asked. "I've been doing all the talking. Tell me about you."

"Well . . . uh . . . " I felt embarrassed. What about me? My life seemed so boring to describe and yet to me it was rich and many-splendored.

"I'm from this town, didn't go to college, married young. My husband was with the National Parks Service. We had a son together named Sam. He's seventeen now and already in college. He's a good boy. Four years ago, when Sam was thirteen, my husband was killed in an accident, hit on the head by a tumbling rock. Now I live with my cat and dog, write stories, sell some. I grow roses and vegetables. I produce soup, sell some of it. I run ... "

"And these four years you've been alone, you haven't fallen into the promiscuity pit?"

"No. Is it a pit?"

"It's a canyon."

He looked at me in a nice way, almost tenderly it seemed. "You're a good woman," he said. "You're serene."

I flushed. "No, no I'm not. I'm quite rowdy at times. It's only fair to tell you."

He smiled and shook his head, disbelieving me.

"Truly. You can ask Maude. She's known me for years. I'm a rowdy and worse."

I wondered if I should tell him I was an adulteress. I didn't want him thinking I was a good woman when I wasn't. He'd been honest with me. He'd told me about being on drugs. That must have been a hard admission. It might have been distasteful for me to hear were it not that my critical faculties were suspended by my smitten state. But I wasn't too goo-goo-eyes to see that his critical faculties were pretty intact. Therefore I couldn't bring myself to say, "Ishmael, I'm an adulteress." It didn't seem appropriate. Or sensible. I was feeling happy, hopeful, loving. I wanted him to love me back. It would be a dumb thing to say. Why not let him think what he wanted to think while he still could. Me too.

However, as we talked on, it emerged that he was searching for God rather than for the woman of his dreams. "I'm seriously considering joining a monastery," he said. "But it's a big decision. Then I wonder if I want to be that formal. Why not simply become a hermit on my own, remove myself from the civilized world and from worldly things, dedicate myself to God? What do you think?"

"That seems too easy, Ishmael. I mean, it seems so easy

to live a good and godly life if you don't have to have any dealings with people, if you remove yourself from all friction and temptation. Not that a hermitage is all fun. It's a hard life, certainly. But I just don't think that was Jesus's idea. Think of the desert fathers, the men who went out on the desert and practiced such ghastly austerities. Their solitude and sun-seared brains deluded them into believing they were in touch with God. Not that they all turned into looneys; there were some men who became holy that way— although I can't think who, offhand."

"The passions of the flesh hamper the growth of the spirit," said Ishmael, and such words coming from such a face sounded so interesting that they made my heart pound. "They set up such a clamor," he sighed. "I want peace."

"Yes, the human heart yearns for peace. But it is one of the great myths that it can be found in solitude. Where can it be found then? I don't know. But it seems to me that if, in life, one can just learn to be gentle . . . Yes, to be gentle . . ."

I faltered and could say no more. I felt embarrassed. He was looking at me admiringly and again I felt I was giving a false impression of goodness.

Even as I was discussing holiness with him, I was entertaining a pretty fierce temptation of the flesh for him. Talk about clamor!

We finished lunch and planned to run together. Soon.

"But I'm slow. It won't be any fun for you."

"It will be fun," he assured me. "I can tell you have a lot of natural speed. You just haven't tapped it. I'll be away for a few days. I'll call you when I get back."

I gave him my phone number.

As I was departing The Splash, Maude took me aside and told me Joe had come in while I was lunching. He had looked around, seen me totally absorbed in the beautiful Ishmael, had turned and left.

I asked Maude, "Did you notice whether, as he was leaving, his entrails were hanging out?"

"No, Miss, I didn't."

3 . . .

As the weeks went by, Ishmael and I established a relationship—a bizarre one. We ran together. We talked a lot on the telephone. We met at places to drink tea or juice and to have deep talks. And that was about the size of it. He did not give me the embraces I was longing for, did not touch me at all. That "gentle gallant way he had of taking me by the elbow" I remembered from the Sunday mountain run turned out to be, for Ishmael, an extreme of physical expression. Nor did he ever come to my house or invite me to his, where, perhaps, some intimacy might have been established if only by virtue of being in a room together. He shunned rooms. Instead we met on trails or at cafés or in some large public room like The Splash—but it emerged that he didn't like bars, being places of intrinsic evil. Many places were evil to Ishmael and many people too. Women were distinctly evil and likewise anything to do with them. Sex, for instance. Ishmael had O.D.'d on sex and was living chastely toward his imminent monkhood.

Why did I, who was yearning for a warm loving physical relationship, fall for a man who had fallen for God?

Was it because of the mythical meeting? Partly. And I felt intrigued by him. And he was beautiful, which, initially, was a draw. He was smart, had interesting thoughts. It was a pleasure to be with him in many ways and yet . . . he was so cold!

"They used to come pounding on my door at night. It was awful. It became a nightmare."

"They" were the women. And that would be awful. Lust is not a pretty thing when it is like that.

I tried to put myself in his place and imagine being home alone at night and some man coming to my door, full of desire for me, knocking at first, then pounding, then breaking the door down.

Golly, it would be wonderful!

No. It would be wonderful if it were Joe or Ishmael, someone beloved. But not if it were an acquaintance, scarcely known. Or worse, a stranger.

Consider the Rapist.

That was lust at its worst. Or was it? I'd started to read up on rape and discovered it to be a crime of violence more than an act of a man driven by desire.

By understanding rape I hoped to obviate the fear of it, for I continued to fear the County Rapist, once freed of the dread of cancer. It had struck me as so pitiful that the only way to be free of the rape dread was to replace it with a larger, more malignant one. I was determined to free myself through understanding. And yet, maybe my moving toward Ishmael was simply a way to free myself from loneliness and therefore fear. If so, that was not a good way. That was not strengthening myself from within, even if I got Ishmael within me—which it didn't look like I would.

To get back to my relationship with Ishmael, if he wanted to move monkward, why was he interested in me?

Because he thought I was a "good woman," and I did not discourage the idea.

I figured that by hanging out with me he would get a good sense of the person I was soon enough. After all, one could say anything about oneself, but one's life and being were the only true example. "By their fruits ye shall know them."

However, I continued to be on my best behavior with him. If someone wants to put you on a pedestal, it is tempting to let him. So I did. I clambered up on the highest pedestal I could find, a virtual stylite I became. It wasn't only that I wanted Ishmael to admire me that I pedestaled it; it was because on my pedestal I felt obliged to stand for all of womankind that he had come to deplore.

Meanwhile, we had wonderful runs together. We went so fast. He wanted me to keep coming to the Sunday runs so I trained up for them during the week, running all over the mountain, running and gasping, yes gasping at last, for I was anaerobic all the way—trying to keep up with Ishmael, who was running easy.

We went down the trails like thunderbolts. Often I fell, but I learned not to cry. I learned to fall well, to roll with it, and get up again quickly, and not examine my injuries until later.

Ishmael sometimes picked me up and wiped me off and told me I was all right. Body contact! That was probably why I fell—so he would pick me up, so his strong arms with their elegant tracery of runner's big veins would grasp me for a minute and for a second I would be close enough to his breast to hear *ka thump, ka thump*, the incredibly loud, slow, beat of his runner's heart.

Maude disapproved. "The marathon is in three weeks and you have not done any distance. You should have about four twenty-milers under your belt by now and you have not done one!"

"But it's so far, Miss! It's so boring! I can't go fast for that distance. I have to plod along."

"Your body has to accustom itself to the long distance. You can't spring it on your body the day of the marathon. Your metabolism has to have accommodated by then."

"Also," she glared at me, "It's bad to keep running on the mountain. You should be running every day on pavement. The marathon is on a road. There's a big difference. Pavement is harder."

"I know," I wailed. "It's such a pounding on the body. Such a punishment. I love the mountain. The trails are like velvet. The views are breathtaking. Every step is so interesting."

"Velvet trails!" Maude snorted. "Look at you! You're a mass of bruises from those velvet trails. You look like you've been mugged."

Maude looked at me seriously, then said more gently, "What's up with you and Ishmael anyhow?"

"Well his penis isn't, that's for sure."

"I don't think he's right for you, Miss."

"I don't either, Miss. How's your love life?" Maude had the same problem as Ishmael of suitors pounding at her door. But she liked it. She gave me a rundown on them all.

"How's Mack?" she asked.

"He's fine. I haven't seen much of him recently. I imagine he's hot in pursuit of the Rapist. He'll get him too."

4 . . .

*F*inally the day came when I showed Ishmael my true colors. It began when I met him in the meadow from whence we were going to run a ten-mile loop. He was sitting on a log in the pensive position of Rodin's *Thinker*, elbow on knee, chin on fist. I touched him. I came up to him and stroked his head, running my fingers lightly over, not through, his curls, resting my hand briefly on his neck. The entire gesture took only seconds.

But first, I'll describe Ishmael. What is beauty? Often it hasn't to do with perfection of features but of a happy conjoining of features and expression. However, Ishmael's features *were* perfect. His hair! Few men have wonderful hair. How often does one see a man and think, what hair! Almost never. His hair was chestnut brown and glossy. It shone! Curled! Thick, crispy curls—a shining helmet of curls set on a noble head. A fine brow, defined temples. Definition was the key for his brow, his lids, the modeling of his lips, clearly defined as if drawn by a master hand in outline, then filled in by it with subtle color as in the coloring of his eyes, which were green, brown, or blue, shifting opaiescently. His lips were red and his teeth strong, white, and regular.

And the man was an athlete, a man who was always testing the limits of his strength, a man with toughness of mind and with a mind that was wrestling with the problems of life and morality so that all this was expressed in his face by the line of his jar, the firmness of his lips, the premature creasing of his brow. Ergo, it was an interesting face as well.

Or did I color it interesting? Was my own mind the master hand that drew and colored the beauty of Ishmael?

Howbeit—I touched him that day in the meadow. It was an impulsive gesture, not premeditated, nonsexual. It was a gesture of affection. Motherly, even. Feeling moved by the way he was sitting and thinking, I reached out to him responsively, as if to comfort. It was a gesture that I might have made to my son, Sam.

He repulsed me. He pulled his head away, stood up suddenly. "Don't do that," he said. "Come on. Let's go." He started running and I fell in behind. I was extremely hurt. I felt vile. I felt as if my touch were vile.

Usually I chattered happily as we began to run, since we run slowly at first, warming up. But this time I was very quiet.

He was not insensitive. After a mile or so he moved back beside me, which means that he slowed enough for me to draw abreast of him, but the impression was one of his drifting back to me. Running is strange that way.

"Don't feel hurt with me," he said. "What is rejection? It is only the ego feeling hurt. Let's get out of our egos. And be free. We can transcend all this physical stuff. When you think of the love of God, what do these human relationships matter? Human emotions are so shallow and meaningless. It is stupid to feel hurt. Let's rise above these petty feelings. Huh, Ronda? What do you say? Say something."

I said something. I said no.

"No," I said. "I'd rather remain a feeling, open-hearted person, vulnerable to rejection and hurt, than detach myself from all feeling and caring, than armor myself off from vulnerability, becoming in the end one who is unable to feel

love. I'm a lover!" I shouted, having to shout because he was
pulling ahead again and I was glad he was because it made
me feel good to shout all these things out at the top of my
lungs. "I'm a woman of feeling and that's the way I want to
be! Love of God has to begin with love of human beings, not
with rejecting them!" I yelled after him. "I'm glad I feel
hurt. I'm glad I *feel!*"

After a while he drifted back to me again. "I haven't
armored myself off."

"You certainly have!" I said indignantly—and hoarse-
ly. "Golly, I just make an affectionate gesture to your head
and you think I'm after your whole body."

That was true. Everything I said was true. Also I truly
was after his whole body. But I didn't want to make love to
him so as to have him. I wanted to express my good feelings
for him. Isn't that what lovemaking is, an expression of love
and tender feeling? Isn't the act of love a transcendent
experience in itself? It was with me and Joe—a celebration
of feeling, a joining. Imagine one body actually entering
another, the other receiving it, holding it fast to her with
arms and legs wrapped tightly around. What closeness!
Only the human animals join so close: heart to heart, mouth
to mouth. See how that sets us and it apart so that it isn't only
sex, Ishmael, it isn't rutting.

While I was thinking all this I sort of forgot about
Ishmael, but then, attracted by odd sounds, I looked up to
see him running along, gesticulating wildly, talking to himself, although I couldn't make out any words.

Maybe I'd been doing that too as I mulled over these
matters. Maybe I, too, had shouted and waggled my arms
like a lunatic. He looked quite crazed.

I hastened over the trail, calling, "Ishmael, are you
okay? I'm sorry I shouted at you. Of course you're a feeling
person. I just don't think feeling desire for someone is such
a bad thing. I think it's a high caliber of feeling. Sublime
even. Ishmael," I choked from oxygen debt, "shall we stop a
minute? Can you hear me?"

"What? What? Forget it. Let's just run, okay? Man, can't we just run? Huh? Can't we!"

"Sure, that's fine with me."

We just ran. Although I was sorry to have upset Ishmael, it felt great to be off my pedestal.

Ishmael still looked disturbed but it was strange because while looking and sounding upset he also seemed somehow gleeful.

We finished the loop and then he seemed himself again—whatever *that* was. I realized that the feelings of love for him that I had conjured up out of my wasted heart had dissipated. But I still felt affection and desire and even a little concern.

5 . . .

Then my son, Sam, came home for spring vacation! "Hi, old lady," he greeted me in his voice that was so deep it sounded trapped in his throat, struggling to get out, struggling so hard that the fewer words he could bring to a sentence, the easier. He was a real child of California: blond, blue-eyed, tan even in early spring. His body was whippet-thin, consisting of bone, muscle, sinew, and about five percent body fat, ideal for a male runner. He stood five feet nine inches and weighed a hundred and twenty, having five inches and fifteen pounds on me. We were the same body type with the same long fingers, legs, and toes but I was darker of hair and eye. His features and coloring were his father's, and there was nothing of Virginia Woolf about him.

At seventeen he had a little fuzz on his upper lip but not serious enough to shave about, and he seemed always to be going around with a semierection. Men are so lucky, or so unlucky, that their sex looks the way it feels. Ours is so hidden. We can be feeling semiswollen but nobody can see and want to help out about it.

Sam didn't think Blue was looking well. "He's so thin," he said. "He seems weak."

"Well, he can't act like a puppy all his life. He's finally calmed down is all—after fifteen years. He's getting it all together at last, mellowing out (in the jargon). It's better to be thin than fat. 'The thin rats are the fat rats' pallbearers.' We're a thin family. Do you think I'm too thin, Sam?"

"Pretty much—too thin.'"

"I asked Ishmael—he's my new running friend—if he thought I was too thin and he said, 'You look like a runner, not like a normal woman at all. You look great,' he said, 'really emaciated!' I believe he meant it as a compliment but it didn't turn out that way. Runners' perceptions of beauty are distorted. I've been getting my miles in, though, and I seem to be getting fast at last. As for this marathon . . . " I sighed.

The marathon was in two days. Sam was going up with me to Weott but wasn't going to run, since it conflicted with his training for spring track. Maude and I were going to an inn near the marathon route, and Sam and his friend, Dan, were going to camp out and be on hand. Mack, as it turned out, wasn't going at all.

"I don't see why you're running a marathon," Sam said. "You're not a long distance runner."

"Just to say I did it, I guess. Something to tell my grandchildren."

"They're going to be so tired of hearing about it. Here comes Grandma with her old marathon story, they'll say. Their eyes will start to glaze over from boredom."

"How come you lock the doors now?" Sam asked later, peering at me over yellow roses and pale flames of candles as we carbo-loaded lasagna. "You never used to do that. There's nothing here to rob."

"Well, there's this County Rapist. He's struck five times, once in this neighborhood. I don't know why I'm so nervous about him but I am."

"He could get into this house so easy."

"Thanks a lot."

"Well, what's the point of locking the doors if you leave the windows open?"

"They're only open a little way. I need the fresh air. And Moby has to get in and out. The locked doors are just a symbol, I guess. It makes me feel secure."

Sam shook his head. "Seems like you've gone a little crazy since I went away. Pretty much—gone crazy."

After supper we resolved to make some chocolate-chip cookies but we were out of flour. Sam said, "I'll go see if old Mack has some."

"If he's not home, he leaves his key under the reddish rock in the pot of his bonsaied Monterey cypress. But leave him a note that you took it."

When he didn't come back in a while, I figured he and Mack were visiting so I, too, went on down to Mack's place.

They were sitting together at Mack's table. Mack had made some brownies and the two of them were scarfing them up, talking away in the monosyllabic way that men do, and managing to get a lot said, in the way that men do.

"How's Jannie?" Mack was inquiring about Sam's girl friend.

"To the dump," Sam said. Only he said it in one word, with a flick of the tongue—tothedump, looking rather pleased with himself.

"Why?" Mack asked. "She was real pretty. And nice too. What was the matter with her?"

"She was weird. But not interesting-weird, weird-weird."

"I hope you were kind," I said, motherly. "This is probably the first of many dumpings you'll do in your life, but remember, it's possible to be kind so that girl doesn't feel too bad, maybe even feels good. It's not what you do so much as how you do it." I said, showing how long it takes a woman to say something even when she's not eating brownies at the same time. "It's a question of style."

"I know."

Everything I tell Sam he already knows.

"Tea?" asked Mack.

"No, thanks." I sat down and dug around in the brownie pan. "I went to hear this lecture on rape," I said.

"What'd you do that for?" Mack asked, disapproving.

"Well, I didn't want to go but I did. I want to understand about it. This journalist was addressing California Press Women on the subject. She herself was raped by that East Bay Rapist, Stinky."

"Yeah, she was an angry black woman *before* she was raped," Mack said.

"What'd she say?" asked Sam.

I sighed heavily. "Well, she was in the man's power for three hours, terrorized by him. She's still amazed that she didn't lose her sanity. Nevertheless, afterward, she had to learn everything over again—how not to be afraid to go out on the street or into her house, how to just get through one day. She said you look like the same person from the outside but internally you are destroyed. Not just because of the physical abuse, but because you've been made powerless. For three hours her life depended on the whim of this man. Blinded, held at knife point, dominated, forced to participate in her own humiliation, reaching the terrible understanding that at best she was unable to protect the most intimate part of herself from this stranger—at worst, her life. She explained that the sex act itself isn't the motivating force of the rapist. He wants to terrorize and dominate and sex is his instrument of violence because it is the most terrifying to a woman. She sees rape as an extension of sexism, the extreme of misogyny and sexism. She says all of our lives are circumscribed by rape—that there is so much physical abuse against women, it's frightening."

Mack shook his head. "That just isn't true. Men don't

want to hurt women. I don't know one man who would want to hurt a woman, who would hit a woman. That's a rare man. There are as many men who would abuse a woman as there are women who would torture children, and that's not very many."

"But the men who do abuse or rape do it repeatedly. Stinky has raped sixty-two women and still hasn't been caught!"

"That's right, but it's still rare."

"But the fear of it isn't rare. The fear *does* circumscribe our lives. A woman *is* far frailer than a man. Somewhere out there is a man who wants to hurt her or rape her. Not just out there; he wants to come into her home, into her bed!"

"Calm down now."

"Take is easy, Mom."

I stood up. "Okay. I'm going to sleep now. And then, in a couple of days, I think I'll just go and run a marathon."

6 . . .

On Gramps' Night, before leaving for the marathon, the old people presented me with a T-shirt made especially for me to run in. In big blue letters on a yellow ground was printed RONDA'S SOUP SERVICE. Embroidered underneath, in many-colored threads, were the words: *It's when she's running, she's really cookin'*. That was the front of the shirt. The back said, GO, RONDA! and had every one of their names embroidered underneath.

7 . . .

*T*he first fifteen miles of the Avenue of the Giants Marathon were terrific. I sailed along, averaging an eight-minute-mile pace, even though I stopped at every aid station for water. I made friends and lost friends as people moved up alongside me or dropped back to me. There was a lot of talking the first ten miles, a feeling of festival and camaraderie, but then the runners began to get awfully silent, like a group of people at a party who have just heard some terrible news so that all the gaiety drains out of them and they realize they're tired and drunk and don't even like each other as much as they'd thought and it's time to go home.

After fifteen miles I could feel my pace begin to slacken. I knew I'd gone out too fast. The idea had been to run a nine-minute-mile pace steadily all the way, but I'd felt so good I couldn't resist moving out briskly. Now I don't feel so good. I knew that at twenty miles there was to be a turnaround, so there would be six miles of backtracking to the finish. At eighteen miles I thought, I'll just get to the turnaround and then it will be like the horse returning to the stable; high-stepping, high-hearted, tail flowing, homeward bound to the comforting stable, the hay, and the grain.

However, by the turnaround, those last six miles had assumed insuperable proportions, and by proportions I don't mean just elongated distance, I mean height and breadth as well. They weren't simply something to run across, they were things to get over or around or through. The miles loomed up solid and palpable as edifices. But that just sounds as if they were three dimensional instead of two. They weren't. They were *four* dimensional, containing time as well—the whole space-time continuum schmear, much heralded by Einstein in his theories.

Talk about pain!

The "hitting the wall" metaphor that marathoners use is good as far as it goes, but it doesn't contain the understanding that you still keep going regardless. You do not remain there on the wall as an eternal bas relief.

Instead, imagine me running along the road and gradually sinking down into the macadam. But still running. First my feet disappear, then my calves, knees, thighs, buttocks, and so on until my whole body, except the head (the head is the only thing that doesn't hurt), is actually *in* the road. But still moving, still running. Only it is like wading. Having to push through it all. Pushing aside not just the crust of macadam but everything underneath: dirt, stones, rubble, roots. Does that sound painful enough? Do you get it? I don't think so. I don't think my analogy really works. Darn.

Okay. Talk about lactic-acid buildup!

Did you ever hear of anything eviller-sounding than lactic acid? That's what was happening in truth to my body. What has happened here scientifically is that my body is out of energy. Glycogen depleted. Glycogen is my energy stores. Store's closed. My muscles have reached their limit. The chemical action which creates energy for the muscles by burning sugar there is no longer working. Lactic acid is a waste product of incomplete chemical burn-up and this waste product is fouling up my blood, which isn't getting enough oxygen. Ergo, I am fatigued. I am burned out. My body, with nothing else to draw on, is now eating its own muscles. Ugh! It is all my fault. I did not train the way Maude said I should. It was a dirty trick to play on my body.

I have said that my head didn't hurt, that my head was still traveling above the road. This is true. With my body burned out and used up, all I had left to run with was my head and that is exactly what I was doing. My head was keeping me going. At first it wouldn't oblige. When the massive pain first hit me, all my head would do was cry "Help!"

I spent a little while feeling deeply sorry for myself and

realized that nothing was being accomplished that way. It wasn't moving me along.

People had fallen by the side of the road, were prostrate or stretching or limping or walking. I didn't want to do any of those things; I wanted to finish the marathon. After all, there was the amusement of my grandchildren to consider as well as my self-esteem. So my head kept me going, directing one foot to be put before another in a semblance of a run. Sometimes my body would stop dead at an aid station, drink water, and not want to go again but it hurt so much to stand still and even more to walk that my head got my body back into its run again, moving jerkily forward.

At twenty-four miles my head was exhausted. The stores closed there too. The only thing left was my eyes.

I can't do it, my eyes cried. I know it's stupid to stop when there are only two more miles to go, sob, but I can't do it, I can't.

Then my eyes saw a wonderful sight. Sam.

Sam was standing at the side of the avenue with his friend, Dan. "Hey, Mom," he said, "You're looking great! I can't believe you're still running. You're going to break four hours."

The beauty of those words! The welkin rang! In my whole life I never heard such words: I was looking great, I was still running. I was going to finish the marathon in four hours. Sam said so. Sam, who is not a flatterer of his mother, a sonly sort of son, which made his words seem incredibly magical and wondrous. Extraterrestrial.

But that's not all. Next Sam said—Sam who would not be seen *dead* running with his mother—said, "Would you like us to run you in?"

All my pain was replaced by pure happiness. I smiled and must have said something funny too, or something pleasing, because all the other runners—running grimly along—began smiling too, smiling and talking together, breaking the somber silence of miles, smiling and encouraging each other so that the air around us seemed to bulge with extraterrestrial music and welkin ringing—some angelic Quasimodo at the heavenly bells.

I ran in, Sam and Dan on each side of me. I felt borne aloft, no longer sunk deep in the roots and rubble but airborne between two boys, musical smiles hymnaling all around. And then there was Maude come to look for me and running me in the last mile and Mack too—where had he come from? There was beloved Mack running me in too, and it just seemed like the happiest moment of my whole life.

Later, back at the inn, I stripped off my running clothes and threw myself naked into the Eel River, which had been slipping silverly along the marathon route, looking cool and so inviting. But the Eel is a wild river. The current grasped me in its mighty arms, took me. I surrendered, lay back, and let the River Eel have its will of me. It entered me, enfolded me, turned me this way and that. I assumed every position for it, was passionately swept along. Fighting, I struggled out, walked back along the bank with its bastion of giant redwoods, and threw myself in again. Three times I let the river take me, feeling much elation.

It was a replenishment.

8 . . .

When Sam and I got home two nights later, Moby came to the door to greet us but Blue did not. He heard us and set up a howling from the bedroom. We went there and found him trying to get up from a lying-down position, but only able to raise himself by his front legs.

"He can't get up," Sam said. "What's the matter, old boy? What's the matter, Blue? Come on, you can get up."

Blue whined and rolled his eyes and licked Sam's hand and looked about as pitiful as any dog could possibly look.

"What a faker," I said. "I know his tricks. He's trying to make me feel bad for going off and leaving him. Goddamn dog. He's so bad. You know how he always has to make some emotional display.

"Blue, is this any way to greet a marathoner? Show some admiration and respect. Okay, I'm sorry I left. I'll never do it again. I love you with all my heart and you're the best dog in the whole world."

As I talked, I reached down and lifted Blue's back end off the floor and set him on his feet.

Blue wavered. He took a few steps but his back feet dragged. They weren't planted right on the floor.

"He's just faking," I said.

"Mom, there's something wrong with him. There's something really wrong."

There was something really wrong. His back legs were paralyzed. By the next day he couldn't get around at all, and Sam would have to carry him outside to relieve himself. Indoors we put him on a blanket so we could drag him from room to room to be with us. Left alone, he would howl and howl. We went on for two days like this, put him on drugs, but he was in bad pain. He could not control his bowels or bladder and would lie in his own dirt.

Sam and I took him to the humane society. Sam drove and I held Blue's head in my lap, stroking him. He seemed to have shrunk down to nothing. Sam carried him in and we both stood by while they gave him a shot. It was a nice death. He went off so easy. It only took a second and he didn't even know. He didn't even twitch when the needle went in and then he just closed his eyes and was dead in a second, just as easy and nice as a death could be and Sam and I were right there with him.

Afterward we sat in the car and cried, not just silent tears, we bawled aloud. Reminiscing, we talked about what a terrible dog he'd always been, so overemotional and badly behaved. Only in the last few years had he begun to mature, to stop chasing our car whenever we drove off or, if locked in, to cease breaking up the place in a fit of pique, to give up gnawing through doors or windows to get out and find us. Probably the reason I had such few possessions was not only the yearning for the simple life but so there'd be less for Blue to destroy when the mood was on him.

But all he'd ever wanted in life was to be with Sam and me—to love us and look after us. He was a sensitive and understanding dog—very tuned in to me and to Sam. We mourned him. Finally, sniffling and puffy-eyed, we drove on home, where Moby waited for us grandly on the gatepost of the picket fence, white on white. We lavished him with affection. What a small family we were now.

Then Sam went back to college and it was just me and Moby.

And Gasping

1 . . .

I went into a decline. I was low in heart. I didn't
want to see anyone, didn't want to cook, write, or
run. I *couldn't* run. My feet were too bruised. I think I hurt
them not so much running the marathon as on the rocky
bottom of the Eel River. Probably the combination. When I
had to stand for any length of time, at sink or stove, I put a
cushion on the floor for my feet. Mostly I lay around. I
didn't answer the phone. I didn't want to see Mack or
Maude. I wasn't up to anything, not even malicious mischief.

The life had gone out of me. The juices had stopped
running, dried up. It's too bad, I thought. Just when I am
coming back to life from the blow of Joe, I begin to die again
of . . .of what? Sore feet? Well, yes. Sore feet.

I did rouse myself for Gramps' Night. I didn't want to
disappoint the old people after they'd made me that beautiful shirt and all. I knew they'd be anxious for a marathon
report, and I wanted to tell them about the old runners
who'd been there: Walt Stack, Mavis Lindgren, Doc Spangler, all of them over seventy.

"When I arrived at the marathon," I told them, "it was
just seven in the morning and still freezing. I had on the

shirt you gave me, my shorts, a turtleneck sweater, and my sweat suit. Walt Stack, he's seventy, was standing there wearing nothing but his running shorts and his tattoos. He's a big, burly, muscular man, a hod carrier by profession, a great encourager of women in running. I went up to him and said I wanted to touch him for luck. I did and he was so warm! He just radiated heat like a furnace."

"Probably sweating out his bourbon from the night before," said Gramps, who knew Walt well.

"Could be." I smiled. "Anyhow, I ran with him a lot of the time and it was a kick. He enjoys himself the whole way. Doc Spangler was going for the world record for eighty-one-year-olds, and when he passed Walt they shouted obscene remarks to each other. 'You dirty old bastard, passing me up,' Walt said . . ."

In this way I roused myself to regale the Gramps-Nighters, but it was a great effort, and when they had gone I fell back into my despondency.

One night, about five days after Blue's death, I stood at the stove, on my cushion, watching water try to boil for my Sleepytime herb tea. I wore my Joseph's robe, a rainbow-striped, velour bathrobe I'd gifted myself with in honor of my marathon. To pass the time I read from the tea box. (This was what I'd come to. This was about as deep as my reading went these days, copy off tea boxes.)

"Contents," I read, "Chamomile flowers, spearmint, tilia flowers, passion flowers, lemon grass, blackberry leaves, orange blossoms, hawthorne berries, scullcap, and rose petals."

I smiled for the first time in days. What a wonderful tea. Imagine imbibing such marvels of the earth.

And what words! Whenever did I see such a string of words before? Why, it's a poem. Or it should be a poem. Right away my mind began to move, turgidly at first, then flowing free, then pure white water.

I hobbled to my writing room, grabbed a pen and paper, went to the dictionary, learned herbs, conjured up botanical visions, wrote, rewrote, boiled away two pots of water. Finally, within an hour, I had my poem, my cup of tea, and my life. The juices were flowing once again.

> *Sleepytime Tea*
> *Flowers, grasses, petals, and leaves*
> *are good nepenthe for one who grieves.*
> *Orange, black, lemon, rose*
> *These are the colors to conquer woes*
> *(I suppose)*
> *Chamomile cured Peter Rabbit*
> *Of his bad McGregor habit.*
> *Flowers of passion, tilia too,*
> *Are the antidote for rue.*
> *And lest the mixture seem too raw,*
> *Add cap of skull and thorne of haw.*
> *Boil water,*
> *Let it steep.*
> *Drink slow,*
> *Drink deep.*
> *Let go.*
> *Benefits reap.*
> *Lie down.*
> *Go to sleep.*

Yes, the juices were flowing again, brain and body. I not only felt full of the urge to write, I wanted to see Ishmael.

But now I was sleepy. I shed my robe and donned my nightie. I got into my old oak bed, closed my eyes, and soon was asleep.

I was awakened by a noise. What was it? Was it a sound at the front door? A rapping? Someone gently tapping at my door?

My ears strained. Nothing. But *something* woke me, some sound penetrated my unconsciousness. Should I get up and investigate? I listened. No, nothing. Nothing now. Silence.

Lying on my back, I was up on my elbows in a gawking position, head up on craning neck. I let go, fell back, relaxed, closed my eyes. It couldn't be the Rapist, I thought sleepily, because he never made a sound. A woman never heard him until he was at her bed with a knife to her neck. But maybe his victims were all heavy sleepers. So many women take pills or liquor. Whereas I sleep with the lightness of a drowse, a state only akin to sleep, not full fathomed.

I lifted my eyelids and glanced uneasily at my open window, Moby's window. Moby had been gone all day. The curtains, not fully drawn, moved slightly with the night breeze. Should I get up and close it and lock it just in case?

No, I felt too cozy. And there were my sore feet to consider. Also, if I closed it, I would have to get up again later to let Moby in.

I closed my eyes. Then I heard footsteps. I gasped.

It was unassailably the sound of feet falling on the weeds that grow by my bedroom window. I knew every other night neighborhood sound by heart: walnuts falling, individual dogs passing, the one raccoon, the step of the boy who sometimes crosses my backyard to his house but *never* the side yard by my window, the sound of Moby leaping to the sill. This sound, of feet falling on weeds, did not fit into any of the categories of known night neighborhood sounds.

In a microsecond I had reassumed my gawking, craning position. My hair was standing on end. Not just head hair, pubic hair too.

What to do? I couldn't make a run for it on wounded feet. But I could make it to the window, slam it down, lock it. That would mean going toward the Rapist, not away. Was that wise?

Adrenaline pumping, I was already moving, whether it was wise or not. I threw back the covers, swung my legs down, landed painfully on my feet with a small cry, moved across the few yards to the window, where I could clearly see a shadow against the cotton curtains, the shadow of a tall, strong man.

As I reached for the top of the window frame, two large hands appeared, first on the sill and then on the bottom of the frame to push the window up.

I screamed and fell back. With a bang, the window shot all the way up. I turned and tried to run but my feet would not oblige. I fell to my knees. I began to crawl rapidly across my bedroom floor, a feat that proved impossible to do in a long, voluminous nightgown, for the forward-going knee captured the cloth near the waist and, as the other knee came forward, the first knee on cloth brought my head and shoulders to the floor. I could make no forward motion. I was actually crawling up the inside of my nightgown instead of across the floor.

I could have pulled the flow of material up around my waist and really made a crawl for it, but with a rapist coming at you through the window, naturally the last thing you want to do is show him your bare behind.

Unable to run or crawl, I went for a sideways roll, a trundle, which neatly carried me under the bed. Haven. Let him try tying me to the bedposts here.

All this transpired while the rapist was coming through the window. He was speaking to me but I was screaming and couldn't hear him. Now my screams had subsided, I was only whimpering, and I heard him say, "Ronda, it's me."

What? The voice was familiar. The name was correct— Ronda—that was my name all right. I peeked out from under the bed. It was Ishmael.

"Ishmael!" I rolled back out into the room. He picked me off the bedroom floor like all the times he'd picked me up from the forest floor. But this time he held me in his arms. "I'm sorry, I didn't mean to frighten you."

I was trembling with fear. I held onto him with all my might as a drowning person would a sudden buoy. "I've tried to reach you by phone," he said. "I was worried about you. I began to imagine something horrible had happened at the marathon."

"Oh, I was so scared just now. You can't imagine how scared I was," I mumbled into his shoulder.

"So I decided to come by," he continued. "I knocked at the front door. Then I thought I'd just look in the window to see if you were here, to see if you had got back all right."

He stroked my back soothingly. I was still trembling but it didn't seem from fear. Imperceptibly the tremble had changed. Or maybe it was the same in essence but it felt good instead of bad. What is a tremble anyhow? What does it mean to tremble?

"I came to the window," he said, "and there you were right on the other side of the pane. Ronda, hey!"

I lifted my face to his. I'd already felt his sex begin to swell. I twined my fingers in his hair and pulled his head down to mine. Our lips met. He put his tongue in my mouth. I sucked on it. He put it deeply in my mouth, as if he hoped the rest of him could follow. Seemingly in seconds we both had become wildly aroused. He picked me up in his arms, still kissing me, and carried me to my bed. He lay down with me on top of him. I whipped off my nightie and commenced to undress Ishmael. He assisted me. I began to cry out with passion. He lay me on my stomach and entered my pudenda from behind, taking my breasts in both his hands. Then, without leaving me, he turned me in such a way that I was on my back and he was upright on his knees, my legs on his shoulders. Impaled upon his penis I, and he, seemed to go from one uncanny position to another so that just when I thought I would ecstatically lose myself, I would become detached from the act from pure amazement.

Finally we settled into the immemorial motion until, with glossolalian cries, we completed our union. The windowpanes rattled; black walnuts tumbled from the tree, hitting the roof like a rattle of kettledrums. We were bathed in sweat. That was nothing new. We'd sweated together before but not with our bodies squelching together the while. It was as if we'd both run our fastest mile and then embraced. We were that weak, that wet, that gasping.

He pulled away, up on his arms, shoulders up, then ass up, withdrawing gently. An enormous pool of sperm began to form beneath me.

We both lay on our backs in utter abandonment as if our bodies had been thrown there.

He smiled at me. "Runners *are* stronger."

"I'm weak as a kitten now."

"It's been such a long time for me. Doing without. It felt wonderful."

"Me too. A long time."

I wondered whether a long time for him was a year, a month, a couple of days.

"I haven't wanted to fuck," he said. I winced at the word. "In fact, I've been unable to. To tell you the truth, I've been impotent. Totally turned off. I don't know what happened tonight but I'm glad it did."

"I am too. You can't imagine..." I paused, became thoughtful. "You don't think... I mean... I hope it wasn't my being frightened that excited you?"

"No. No, I think it was the way you held onto me at first, for comfort and protection, like a child, rather than a woman. Not that I'd be excited by a child. It's not that. It's that you were submissive, I guess, not aggressive." He was quiet and said again, "It's been a long time."

What about God, I wondered. I decided not to bring Him up.

Or what about me?

I turned on my side so I could see Ishmael better. "Do you think it might have been that you were glad to see me?"

He looked puzzled. "How do you mean?"

"I mean, mightn't you have felt desire for me because you missed me and were glad to see me again? Because you like me?"

"No, that's not why one fucks."

"You don't think lovemaking is an expression of feeling?"

"No. I do like you. I am glad to see you again. But, hell...you can fuck anybody. You do it because it feels good."

"But obviously you can't fuck anybody, Ishmael, or you wouldn't have gotten turned off. Maybe you had to find somebody you cared about."

"I can see why you'd want to think so."

I was sorry I'd pursued the subject. I was beginning to feel chilled. And it wasn't just that my body was cooling, the sweat drying.

I got up, tottered to the bathroom, washed myself, and put on my Joseph's robe, glad I had something so pretty to appear in. I combed my tangled hair and admired my reflection. Shining eyes and rosy cheeks. Ishmael was not amiss about how good it felt. Why couldn't I let it go at that?

When I came out, I found Ishmael in the kitchen. He had dressed and was making us each a bowl of bananas, strawberries, honey, and cream. "Thank you, Ishmael. What a nice idea."

We ate our fruit, saying little but feeling companionable. Ishmael washed up although I protested. "I love to wash dishes," he said, "I'm very good at washing dishes." He was. When he left a few minutes later, the sink and counters looked nicer than I could remember.

2 . . .

I made myself a cup of tea and planned to go to bed all over again. What an extraordinary night.

I saw that it was just after one A.M. I'd lost track of time. I wondered what time Ishmael had come. It must have been pretty late. How terrifying it had been. Now I knew a little of how these raped women felt. Wow! To have a man at your own bedroom window, *coming through it*!

What if Ishmael came through the window because he is the Rapist?

Oh, come on. I pushed the thought from my mind as soon as it popped in.

Wait a minute, Ronda, just consider it. It won't do any harm to consider it. It would do more harm to repress it.

I wouldn't dream of considering it. What an unkindness to Ishmael.

They why did the thought even come? Just take a minute to look at it, then you can put it away forever.

All right, fair enough.

I got back into bed and propped myself up against the headboard with my pillows. I sipped tea and marshaled my thoughts.

Okay, Ishmael was virtually a pickup. We weren't introduced. The only things I know about him are what he himself has offered to tell me. I don't know any of his friends. The other mountain runners seem to be merely acquaintances, not intimates of his.

It can be said, certainly, that Ishmael has a fear of women which, from my rape reading, I'd learned was sometimes a motivating force. The rapist fears and hates women. A woman is not a real person to him. A woman is to a rapist what a black man is to a Klanner—a nonhuman.

Ishmael had never come to my house before tonight. As far as I knew, he did not even know where I lived. My address was not in the directory. So, if he was the Rapist going his rounds, he could have come here not knowing it was my house.

Did he speak to me before or after he came in the window? I was screaming too hard to tell. It seems to me I can remember him saying, "It's me." But what if, in actuality, he said, "It's you!" amazed to recognize his victim as his friend?

No, I'm sure he said, "It's me." And I'm quite sure he spoke to me before he came in. Although it does seem strange for him to have elected to come by so late. I've been here all day, every day.

But it's true that I haven't been answering the phone.

Yes, let's look at the positive side now.

We've been seeing each other rather regularly for a couple of months. He hadn't seen me for a whole week or been able to reach me. He may have suddenly, spontaneously, decided to seek me out, never even noticing the time of night. Maybe he asked Maude for my address. Of course! He probably did ask Maude.

He is a sensitive person. Because he's been sexually besieged by aggressive, liberated women, he's withdrawn from society. I believe he's been attracted to me since the day in Paradise Produce when I turned away from his beauty rather than move hungrily toward it. He believes me to be a good woman and I am a pretty good one. He likes me, likes to run with me, talk with me, and now he's discovered he even likes to make love to me. (Fuck me?)

In a way, Ishmael has been raped. Women know how to say no to a man and men can accept the no. But men have never had to learn to say no to a woman until recently. And women have not learned to handle a refusal, because they still are under the illusion that they are offering something, whereas in fact they are taking. So they are hurt, indignant, or contemptuous if a man says no to them. They are not gracious in defeat. But most men will not say no, feeling it unmanly or dishonorable or unkind and gradually the whole act becomes repugnant. They are being *forced into intimacy* rather than choosing it. And that is what rape is.

By the same token you could say that because he has been raped he is getting back at women by becoming a rapist, thereby becoming the dominant one again.

Well, I could go around and around with the thing. And it is bootless, because it seems to me that whether Ishmael is a rapist or not, I am committed to him in my heart and that, in any case, he needs my love and affection. A rapist is a person.

Hold on. Could I possibly love a rapist? A rapist is the lowest form of life. It is the foulest crime, perpetrated by the basest person. Could I love a man who had terrified my sisters, who had brought fear into their lives perhaps permanently?

No.

And yet . . . a rapist is a person. He is the man next door. He is the friendly grocer. He is everywhere. He might even be your husband.

3 . . .

Up at the inn the night before the marathon, when Maude and I prepared for bed, I had told her about the rape lecture I had attended. "Since then," I told her, "whenever I talk about rape with a man, Mack for instance, they look horror-struck and say that it is so rare—they know of no men who could do such a terrible act, that it is a one-in-a-million kind of thing. But every woman I talk to knows of at least one friend who has been raped. Even Sam, after my talk with Mack, came and told me his girl friend had been raped and that he knew of two other girls who had!"

"I've been raped," Maude said.

"I mean, just think of it, *three* girls of Sam's acquaintance . . ."

"You didn't hear what I said, Miss. I said, I've been raped."

After a moment of silence, I said, "I heard but I couldn't bear to register it. Maude, I've known you for over twenty years..."

"Frederick Leher raped me," she named her husband. "Before we were married. I was a virgin. He had already asked me to marry him but I wasn't sure I loved him. He was a real catch for me since I was a small-town kid going to a junior college and he was a law-school graduate and rich too. He was visiting me and my family, and one day when I was out, he went through my drawers and found some love letters from an old beau. He became extremely jealous. When I got home and came into my room, he was there. He threw the letters at me. Then he pulled me down, tore off my pants and raped me.

"It was only a matter of seconds. I hardly knew what was happening. It hurt.

"He said I had to marry him now—I belonged to him. And I was defiled for any other man, he said. I believed him. I felt dirty and guilty. I felt *I'd* done something wrong and was even grateful he would take me under his protection.

"My parents were thrilled by our engagement. Before the wedding I told my mother that I didn't love him, that I was scared of him. She turned a deaf ear. It took me ten terrible years to find the strength to get away, and it's taken me many more years to be able to enjoy sex with a man, even to begin to learn to respond to a man."

"My poor friend. I'm so sorry. It's the saddest story I ever heard."

I felt such a welling up of grief for Maude. I'd been away with my husband at different national parks those ten years Maude meant, only coming home every so often for a brief visit. She'd never confided this to me. What good could it have done? Even if she'd come to me before her marriage, could I have helped her then? Or would I, like her mother, have pointed out what a very good catch he was in all other ways—and that was just the way men behaved sometimes.

Probably he'd gone on raping her over the years. No wonder her face was unaccustomed to smiles.

"Now I don't even begin to enter into a relationship with a man until we've had sex together. That's the first thing I want to know about him," Maude said.

"Strange. For me it's the last. But it makes perfect sense. I can see why you'd want to do that. But can a man be tender and affectionate if he hardly knows you? Can you really tell right off the bat like that?"

"Yes. I can tell."

"I've only known two men, Alan and Joe, and they were both wonderful lovers for me. I certainly have been lucky."

"Real lucky. One died and the other dumped you. I don't know how you go through so much suffering and retain your optimistic spirit."

"Life has been very good to me, in its way."

"Because you only see good wherever you look or whomever you look at."

Sipping my tea in the small hours of the morning, I recollected this conversation with Maude. She was right. It was hard for me to see bad in anything or anyone (save for Louise Masterson, for whom my dislike continued unmitigated). From where I lay now, I could not see Ishmael—or what had happened here this evening—clearly. I should not play it as it lay, or as I lay. I should bestir myself and learn more about the County Rapist.

Maybe Mack can tell me more, I thought. I'm sure there's more that Mack could tell me.

Suddenly I remembered him saying that the Rapist was a black man. What a flood of relief went through me. No matter that at the time I didn't believe Mack, wouldn't countenance it. I believed him now.

On the highwater of my relief, I floated off to sleepytime.

4 . . .

The next day, a Saturday, I took my rosy cheeks and shiny eyes to town and sashayed about as best as I could with sore feet. Precognitive powers going full blast, I knew I'd run into Joe, and I did. In the bookstore. I hoped the rose and the shine wouldn't drain away at the sight of him. I wanted him to see me full of life, a woman who had run a marathon and embraced a new lover, all in a week.

My heart melted at the sight of him. Sex with Ishmael had been powerful and erotic, but what a difference there is to the act when it is informed by love. Joe would caress me in such a way . . . speak so tenderly to me . . . use words that . . .

"Hello, Ronda. How are you. How's your writing going?"

He smiled when he asked me that, because I had once told him that no one ever asked me how my writing was going. Since then he always asked me, and it always gave me pleasure when he did.

"Very well, thank you," I answered.

He had on his old, browny-gold corduroy jacket that was the color of his hair. He looked taller and more distinguished than I remembered him. What a very tall man he was. I had to look way up to him. How did he ever fit in my house, in my bed, in me? Maybe in the meantime I had shrunk.

"I'm writing a most absorbing short story now which I shall call 'There In My Festive Breast.' "

"What a bizarre title." Joe looked around uneasily. In fact, he'd been looking about uneasily since he'd first greeted me, and his condition had progressed from uneasy to nervous upon my zestful explanation of the word *breast* placed in festive terms. I saw that, indeed, other people in the store were ogling us as if to say, why is the town mayor discussing festive breasts with this woman?—so he had reason to feel self-conscious.

But it made me mad. I did not like to see Joe worried about other people, perhaps worrying that our innocent conversation in a bookstore would get back to Louise in the form of vile gossip. I did not want him to feel craven. I'm afraid it made me talk even louder.

"It's from St. John of the Cross's poem '*The Dark Night: Songs of the Soul,*' which rejoices at having reached that lofty state of perfection; union with God by the way of spiritual negation." This is the verse:

> *'There in my festive breast*
> *walled for his pleasure-garden, his alone*
> *the lover remained at rest*
> *and I gave all I own*
> *gave all, in air from the cedars softly blown.'*

"Isn't that beautiful? 'In air from the cedars softly blown,' " I repeated lovingly.

"I thought it was St. Francis you adored."

"Yes, but St. John of the Cross is a great poet, which Francis was not. St. John and Emily Dickinson are the two great mystical poets of all time." I looked about. Everyone in the shop was all ears. "Saints," I added vaguely, "are also persons."

"Yes, well . . ."

"They were both equally dedicated to God but St. John must have been dedicated to his art as well, which Francis was not. Nor did he have the talent by a long shot . . ."

Suddenly I found myself wondering if an artist could be a lover too, could dedicate herself to a man and be unfaithful to her art thereby. Maybe my art must be my only lover just as God, in the poem, could be the only lover for St. John. "In the verse I just quoted," I said to Joe, "the line that comes just before '*there in my festive breast,*' is '*the loved one wholly ensouling in the lover.*' Perhaps, from now on, it should

be my lot to become wholly ensouled in my writing." I
looked up at Joe and it seemed to me that I would never love
again, that Joe was my last love.

I fell completely silent. The gathering of book-buying
townspeople had readdressed themselves to the stacks,
doubtless feeling discouraged, feeling that the mayor's conversation, which had begun so promisingly, was no longer
personal and sprightly but had bogged down hopelessly in
quotes. Joe was looking wretchedly down at me.

"I must be going," he said.

"Of course."

"It's been nice talking to you. I'm glad everything's
going well. You look thin, though, and tired. I hope you're
eating enough. Please take care of yourself, Ronda."

Thin? And tired? What of my rosy cheeks and shining
eyes? Thin and tired? What was this? Hold on a minute . . .

He turned to go. I followed him out the door. I wanted
to tell him about Blue.

Together we walked smack into Louise. "I came to
fetch you. We're late," she said, rather grumpily I thought.
Then she saw it was me.

"Hello, Louise," I said, gracious as could be.

She cut me. She turned her face away from me, took
Joe's arm and commenced to walk away. I couldn't believe it.
Women did not behave that way anymore. That went out
years ago. And anyhow, she'd won, hadn't she? She'd got
what she wanted. I was the vanquished one. Couldn't she,
the victor, find it in herself to be kind, to be friendly?

She'd cut me. I was beneath her notice. I did not exist at
all. I was the lowliest insect beneath her well-shod feet.

The blood rushed to my face. I began to tremble. What
a lot of trembling I was doing these days. I still would like to
know more about trembling. I must launch an inquiry into
anatomical tremblings.

Meanwhile, was I going to let her lay me low like this? I
stood there, red of face, my mind a blank. Probably. my

mind was red too, and the whites of my eyes—engorged by the same blood that rushed to my face.

They walked away. Joe did not look back. Slowly, formally, stiff as ramrods, they walked away.

Next to the bookstore was a florist, and the florist had set out terra cotta pots of red geraniums. Or, who knows, they could have been white or blue; I was only seeing red. I made a grab for one. I picked it up and threw it after them with all my might. It almost hit Louise. It fell just a little short, crashing at her heels. She turned and saw what had happened, saw the shards of pottery, the broken, bloody geranium at her feet. Now it was her turn to be red-faced. She looked at me with unutterable hatred. Joe was appalled. I was a half-block away, standing tall, head high, hands on hips. I must have looked good (maybe, even, magnificent!) but I was trembling something fierce from head to toe. I turned and went into the florist to pay for the geranium, thinking:

I did it again, Mack. But I was provoked this time.

Malicious mischief.

Or maybe worse, assault.

My crimes are mounting.

I wonder how many people saw.

Poor Joe.

"*And I gave all I own, gave all, in air from the cedars softly blown.*"

My feet hurt. I feel faint. Did I pay the man for the plant? Yes, I did. Can I make it to the car, to my home? Oh, help me, someone, something . . . if only . . .

5 . . .

I recovered my equilibrium and maneuvered the Honda safely home. As I parked, Moby did not leap upon the hood of the car to greet me, which meant he still wasn't home. Well, he'd stuck around and been so loving after Blue died, stifling his natural tomcatting tendencies so as to be home for me. Probably he just couldn't stand it anymore and had made such a night of it that he was sleeping it off somewhere. I could do with a little sleep myself.

I dragged into the house and fell on my bed in a swoon.

It was late afternoon when I came to. Mack was at my bedroom door.

"Uh?"

"I want to talk to you, Ms. Thompson."

I sat up and patted a place on the bed for him to sit. "Is this an official visit?"

"No, no, just friendly."

"Did you see Moby anywhere?"

"Not for a couple of days. Are you awake now?"

"Yes, I'm awake. Want a beer or anything?" I kept beer in the fridge for Mack.

"No, thanks. Now tell me all about this flower pot incident."

"Oh, God."

Now Maude walked into my bedroom. "I heard you threw a geranium at Joe, right in the middle of the town square. It's unbelievable."

"I believe it," said Mack. "I'm getting so I'll believe anything."

"It wasn't at Joe, it was at Louise. I was provoked. I paid for the pot. It didn't hit her. What's the problem?"

"You just shouldn't ought to do things like that," Mack said. "It makes me feel worried. Damn!" he added for no reason I could see.

"I went to town today, feeling so good; beautiful and renewed is what I felt. It seemed like I was really feeling fine and somehow everything turned terrible all in an instant. Everything got all out of hand. I don't know. I don't want to talk about it if it's okay with you guys. There's nothing to say that I can see. Maude, have you seen Moby?"

"Not for a couple of days."

"If something has happened to Moby I just don't know what I'll do." Tears flooded my eyes.

Maude went to the refrigerator to get wine. I kept wine there for Maude. "Want a beer, Mack?" she called.

"Yeah, sure."

"Juice, Miss?"

"Okay. Thanks."

Mack and Maude hung around a couple of hours keeping me company. We all sat on the bed. I could tell they knew I needed company and that's all they'd really come to do. After a while I got the talk around to the Rapist. "In my rape reading I've found . . ."

Mack rolled his eyes. "Oh Jesus, her rape reading. Now it's her rape reading."

"Never mind," I scowled. "I'm just trying to understand about it."

"You go too far with everything. You don't know when to stop," Mack said.

"Maybe so. But will you please answer me a few things, Mack? I'd be grateful if you would."

"Okay, shoot."

"Do you feel confident that the Rapist is black?"

"One woman saw his hands before she was blindfolded. They were black hands."

"They could have been gloves."

"No, she felt them."

"Maybe tanned hands?"

"She said black and we tend to believe her because she's black."

"I'd give her testimony more credence too. Good."

"Now you want him to be black."

"Tell me what he does. It's important to me to know."

Luckily Mack had had a few beers by now. "None of the women said he penetrated them himself. He used an object. This was after a lot of talk and humiliation and ... uh ... cunnilingus."

"Which is that, Maude? I always get them confused."

"That's the man licking the woman, Miss."

I felt absolutely certain now about Ishmael. This just wasn't his style at all. Especially when you thought of the tying-to-the-bedposts aspect, because Ishmael appeared to especially enjoy assuming all those different positions. He liked plenty of movement and action and serpentine entanglement. And we hadn't had oral sex at all—not that I didn't hope we would—and there was pretty convincing proof now that the man was black.

"Has he struck again?" Maude asked.

"The newspaper article flushed out some more victims who hadn't reported it at the time. It looks like he's struck at least twelve times. Some of the women got cut up a little but so far, nobody hurt."

"Nobody hurt, Mack?" I asked. "Nobody *hurt*? Think about what you just said."

"I know, I know. I take it back. They were hurt. They were all badly hurt. I know. Jee-sus! Rape readings. I'm going home. Take it easy." He had his finger out at me again. "I mean it. Take It Easy."

"I really like that Mack," Maude said after he'd gone. "Why doesn't he come beating on my door like all the others?"

"He's too busy being a policeman. He loves being a policeman. You know he spent all those years working in his father's company, manufacturing trashy plastic furniture, hating every minute of it. Then, four years ago, he decided to be a policeman. He quit success, went to the academy, became a rookie. Now he's passed the sergeant's exam. He's so good he'll probably be made lieutenant but he doesn't want that because he'd end up back behind a desk again. I think he'd like to be a detective. Good old Mack. He's had hard times. His father won't speak to him now and his wife, of course, left him because a cop husband has no status."

"She's a fool," said Maude.

I shrugged. "Everyone wants different things, I guess."

"What do you want?"

"Well, Miss, I want to be able to write my stories, look after Sam as long as he needs me, love a good man—maybe—or maybe I'll become wholly ensouled in my art . . ."

"Holy what?"

"Never mind. And I want to be able to be an uncowed runner of mountains, live in a simple sunny house with a vegetable patch and a bush of yellow roses and I want to learn to be a good person, both brave and gentle and that's all, really. It's not so much somehow, but, I feel it all going, all slipping away: first Joe, then Blue, my feet, even Sam has gone, now Moby. I know in my heart that Moby's gone for good." I paused and tears filled my eyes. "Moby's gone looking for Blue . . . and found him."

Maude was sympathetic. She put her arms around me. "Your feet are going to get better." That's all she could promise me.

"I hope so. At least if I could run again. It's so terrible not being able to run."

"I know," she comforted. "How's Ishmael? Have you seen him?"

"Well, sort of. He's fine. I like Ishmael." I found I could not tell Maude about the previous night. It was too weird and too soon. I had to let it sit awhile before I could speak of it, before I could recount it to Maude. make a story of it. It was too close, still, and too weird.

Not that I worried that she would think he was the Rapist. I'm sure that wouldn't enter her mind. It had only entered mine because I'd been so obsessed about the damned Rapist and so scared. Anyone else would accept that a friend, not getting an answer at the door, had come to the window. Anyone else would accept that without getting all freaked out about it, without overreacting: screaming, crawling, rolling under the bed . . .

Anyhow Mack had completely put my mind at rest. The only thing in his account that could at all give me pause was that bit about the Rapist's impotence, because Ishmael had spoken of that and how did a man know that about himself unless he'd tried lots of times and failed.

All I really had to do now was ask Maude if Ishmael had gotten my address from her yesterday and then I could put all this nonsense out of my mind forever.

But somehow we got off on other things and I didn't ask Maude and she went away. No matter, I thought. I'll just ask her the next time I see her.

6 . . .

*B*efore going to sleep that night I tried to come to grips with the Geranium Incident. I had told Mack "no problem" but it was a problem, a serious one. I did not like losing control like that. I did not like to think that so much feeling about Joe and Louise still inhabited me. I believed that I was recovered, that I had relinquished him. It was true she had provoked me, but why did I let myself be provoked? Why didn't I just smile and shrug and say to myself that if she wanted to behave like an asshole that was her problem? Why couldn't I rise above all these base human emotions?

Because I'd told Ishmael that day, shouted at him, that I didn't want to rise above them, that I wanted to remain open and vulnerable, a feeling person. I guess what I meant was that I wanted to feel the good things and not the bad things. Now I saw that that was not humanly possible.

What if I had hit her? What if the pot had struck her in the temple and killed her? It was terrifying to think of. There was no way I could exonerate myself from what I had done today. As well, I had humiliated myself in front of her and Joe and the whole town.

That didn't matter. Not at all. And I couldn't honestly say I regretted doing it since no harm had been done. What mattered was that I had this uncontrollable maliciousness in me. This wasn't the me I aspired to be. And it was no good promising myself I'd be better and never do it again, because I seemed to have no say over these actions. I just did them.

I sighed.

My heart felt very heavy there in my festive breast.

You Try To Prevail

1 . . .

*E*nter Joey Horgan. Why, simply because the man had taken a picture of me, did he think that bought him a ticket into my life? Why did *I* think so?

He called me a few days after the Geranium Incident.

"Hey," he said, "this is Joey Horgan," he said, as if I should know the name instantly. It was a voice that carried extraordinary confidence, not bravado, and it only took four words for me to recognize this quality. This is Joey Horgan, he said as one might say, this is the President of the United States.

"I'm glad to hear it," I said dryly, being at my desk in the middle of a thought process.

"Joey Horgan the photographer," he added magnanimously. "Is this Ronda Thompson?"

"Ronda Thompson, the writer," I replied, unable to resist.

"Oh? Is you a writer?"

"Yes."

"That's very interesting. What sort of things do you write?"

Nobody ever asks me that and I immediately warmed to the man and wanted to tell him about all my stories in detail but it occurred to me to ask first, "Mr. Horgan, why are you calling? What can I do for you?"

"Oh yeah, that's right. I got this picture of you. It's a very remarkable picture. I'd like for you to see it. I took it at the marathon, right?"

"You mean the finish line picture? I ordered that when I registered. Doesn't that just come in the mail?"

"I don't know nothin' about that. All I know is I got this incredible picture of you and I found out who you was because of the number you was wearing, see?"

"How did you happen to bother to take my picture? I certainly wasn't one of the faster women to immortalize."

"I was shooting at the twenty-four-mile point. I was into the agony of the experience, you know? It was very interesting there at the twenty-four-mile point because there you get the runners who are still going, right? But they're not finished yet, so they ain't elated like they're going to be at the twenty-six-mile, three-hundred-and-eighty-five-yard point. They're hurtin'. Bad. Wow, you should see some of these pictures. But that's intriguing to me that you're a writer. I'd like to read something you wrote."

"Well, if you go to a library or dentist's office and find a back issue of *Redbook*, try August 1975 for instance . . ."

"What're you writing right now?"

"A short story called 'There In My Festive Breast.' "

"Great title!"

My heart pounded with pleasure at his reaction. Now that *could* buy a ticket into my life. But then he said:

"Maybe you need a picture of yourself for the book jacket of a book of your stories, right?"

"Wrong."

"What's the story about? The breast one? Running?"

"No, it's about, well, I suppose . . . God."

"Wow!" His voice, which sounded continually excited anyhow, as well as wonderfully mellifluous, really lit up now. "Wait'll you see this picture! I'll be right over."

"Wait a minute!"

He'd hung up. He must have gotten my address from my marathon number too, I thought bitterely. It's not right for them to give out that information. If he saw my registration he knows my age as well. And my height and weight. Even my AAU number. It's not right.

Nevertheless I was curious to see this picture. It seemed that this was something more than simply a photographer wanting to make a buck by selling a picture. Something about the picture made him want to know more about me, meet me. It couldn't be my resemblance to Virginia Woolf because there was no way I could have looked like her then. Virginia Woolf never sweated. To my knowledge she was never seen in shorts and singlet or photographed with her mouth open.

After a few minutes I got up from my desk to go and close the front door so this guy wouldn't think I always left the door open which, on nice days, I always do, and he was there, already, on the stoop, a short, dark, beefy man dressed in high-heeled boots, jeans, a scarf tied pirate fashion around his head and, all unbuttoned, one of those bright Hawaiian silk shirts that surfers like to wear.

But he was not a surfer, and not a runner either. He was a photographer. He was all eyes. He had big, round, bulging eyes that swallowed up whatever they looked at. They sucked you in, swirled you around in his brain and genitals and ejaculated you out.

"Yeah! All right!" he said, giving me this look that got his eyes more and more engorged. "This is something! This is really something. Something for sure is happening here. I gotta take *more* pictures of you."

He walked by me, shouldered by me, and went through the house; the writing room, living room, bedroom, and kitchen. "Yeah. I see," he kept saying. "I see." He even said, "I get the picture," a phrase I somehow wouldn't expect from a photographer. And then he was back with the big searchlight beam on me again. "Wow. This is too much to believe."

He was honestly excited. I understood exactly the creative excitement he was going through and I reverberated to it wholly, but I wasn't going to be drawn in. I wasn't used to strangers in my home and it made me uneasy. I don't like strangers. I don't like people to thrust themselves into my life. I like to choose my friends, maybe one every five years, and just keep them forever.

So I tried to look weary and put-upon and to say crisply, "Mr. Horgan, you said on the phone you had a picture to show me."

"Call me Joey."

"I don't want to call you Joey."

"Why not?" he asked, amazed.

I didn't tell him. I just said, "The picture?"

"But why don'tcha want to call me Joey?"

"Look, I don't want to call you Joey and I don't want you in my house and I don't even want to see the picture anymore."

"What's the matter with you? Relax, willya? Willya please relax? It's okay. You don't have to call me Joey. I don't give a fuck what you call me. Just sit down." He shoved me into a chair. "Sit down a minute, willya, while I get out this picture?"

He opened a black plastic zippered case. "Look. Here. Here it is. See that? Do you *see* that?"

"Good God! I don't believe it. You touched it up."

"I swear." He put his hand on his heart. "I swear to God. Give me a Bible. I never touched it. You can look at the negative. I never done a thing to it."

It was a black-and-white picture of me running along, slowly, very slowly, and over my head was a halo.

I felt chilled. My skin crawled. It shivered. (Trembled?)

"I cropped it. That's all I did. Here's the whole picture. Enlarged."

There I was, same picture of me running along slowly with a halo over my head but now Dan and Sam were on either side of me and there were about four other people in the picture too and every single person was smiling and it all came back to me—that incredible moment. The halo didn't appear as an actual ring or circle. What it was was a sort of nimbus of light around my head.

"Okay, I think I can explain this, Joey."

He smiled. "That's good."

He meant it was good I had called him Joey. The explanation he didn't care about. But I did.

I told him about my marathon. The pain. The mental misery. The unutterable joy at seeing Sam. The further joy of his willingness to run me in. Total happiness.

"So here's what I think happened," I went on. "I was sweating a whole lot anyhow. Sweating is glowing. In the old days they used to say, 'women don't sweat, they glow.' So I was glowing away and then came this unexpected burst of happiness which, of course, also makes one glow, and that combined with my running glow to send a wave of, well, of water really, precipitation, humidity, a cloud of humidity upward from my body and then the sunlight hit it in such a way . . . the same principle as a rainbow, you understand . . . Plus the fact that on hand you have a photographer who sees more than normal people do and well—there you have it!"

I sat back, pleased as I could be. I had rationalized the uncanny. I was in control. "Tell me something. Do you see anything like a nimbus of light around me now? Tell me honestly."

"Yeah, I do."

"You do?"

"Nuthin' like in the picture but yeah, of course I do."

I felt the chills coming on again. But I recovered and said, forcing a smile, "Probably you see varying degrees of light around everyone, right?" (I was talking like him now.) "Isn't that right?"

"No, wrong. I don't. I never have."

"You're lying through your teeth."

"I never have. You're the first one. And I'll show you

something else you didn't notice." He picked up the picture and pointed to my feet. "You're running very slowly, right? Cause you're hurtin' like hell. People running slowly—they got at least one foot planted on the ground—usually part of the other foot too. When runners are really moving, they're stretched out, they're in flight, both feet off the ground. Running slow, never. But look at your feet. Both off. Both! Know why? You're levitating." He grinned. "That's why."

"It's an illusion." I pointed. "That foot's on the ground. There."

"No it ain't. See the shadow. If it was on the ground, the shadow would be connected to the foot. It ain't. The shadow starts here. You're levitating. You're glowing. You're a saint. You're a running saint. And that's what I'm callin' the picture. 'The Running Saint.' "

2 . . .

"*I* am not a saint. I've got witnesses!" I was up on my feet now, flinging myself about the room. Joey watched me with interest. "Why only the other day I almost killed a woman, a nice woman of the town who never did me any harm. If anything, I had harmed her . . ."

I stopped; what was I saying? Why did I have to prove myself to this man? Or disprove myself, as it were. Who was he? Nobody. All he had was a tricked-up picture of me. That was all. That was *all*.

"Look," he said reasonably. "If you put this picture on your book jacket and your book is about God, you'll have a best-seller."

"I don't write books. I don't *have* a book. It's just a story I mentioned, a half-written story."

"We'll get you a book then."

"You don't understand at all—not one thing." I looked at him in wonder.

"I understand what sells and this picture will sell your book. You'll be rich!"

"I don't want to be rich."

"What are you? Some kind of a saint?"

"And even if there were a book I wouldn't use this picture if my life depended on it because it's too embarrassing. It's a crazy picture, a flukey, goony, lunatic picture."

"You'll see how far that attitude will get you. You get no say about the jacket at all. I know the business. But let's make a deal. Maybe I won't sell this picture of you if you'll let me take some more pictures of you."

"What kind of deal is that?" I squealed. "Then you'll have more pictures of me to sell."

"Look, don't you see that I just want to photograph you and this house here and your life? Please! I got to do it."

"No. I'm sorry, I can't let you do that. It's my life and you would be taking it from me somehow. Like primitive peoples think that a camera captures their soul. Keeping my life simple, private, and unencumbered is what allows me to do my work. You must understand this, Joey, because you're an artist too."

Joey was an artist but the difference between us was that he was a fanatic. While my art was important to my life, an integral part of it, I felt that with Joey, his art was all. His life didn't matter: where he lived, who his friends were, what he ate, whether there were flowers on the table—none of that mattered.

"Just think about it is all I ask. Right now you're over-reacting to that picture, which I can see why it threw you. It's unique and tremendous. But think it over. Think about the benefits. I'm Joey Horgan. Ask around about me. There are people on their *knees* to have me take them."

"Take them!" I exclaimed. "Aha! Notice that you said take them. That's exactly what I'm talking about. I won't be taken."

He rolled his eyes, blew out his cheeks, shook his head (talk about overreacting), and said, "Look, never mind about all that crap; it don't mean nothin'. What we're talking about here now is not just a book-cover picture but a whole, entire book of pictures. An exhibition. We're talking Museum of Modern Art."

"I don't care if you're talking Louvre. It's no deal."

"I'm going now."

"I'm delighted to hear it."

"Take it easy, girl. I'll see you later—when everything's cool."

He left.

I shut the door.

Locked it.

3 . . .

A̲t Gramps' Night now, the subject was rape. Disease and running had gone by the board. It was as if they'd just discovered the County Rapist. No, it was as if they'd been given permission to talk about it; probably because he'd struck again, the fourteenth time, and the papers were doubly full of it.

The women talked about it, that is. Old men, like young men and middle-aged men, did not contribute much to rape discussions, fell uncomfortably silent. I began to understand that, for men, it was deeply troubling. It was, of all the crimes, a man's crime. It was their province. Who of them could look into their hearts and not see rape's dark shadow there, from some inadmissible moment in their lives or consciousness?

"What about prostitutes?" one old man shouted out

confusedly, as if to show that there were bad women in the world too.

"I'll tell you an amazing thing about prostitutes that I read just recently," I said to them all. "Eighty-five percent of all prostitutes are either incest or rape victims."

"Sons of bitches," Gramps muttered to no one in particular.

I took him literally. It made me pause. I realized, Yes, all rapists were sons of women. Where does the terrible wrong begin? And where, oh where will it end?

4 . . .

*D*ays passed. I kept my bedroom window open for Moby but he never came through it. Ishmael did. He didn't come for about five days and then he began to come regularly. What he did during those five days I don't know. Did he soul-search? Pray? Did he try his newfound potency out on other women? I don't know. I know I was happy when he returned. And if he wanted to keep coming through the window, that was okay too. It seemed to work for him. Maybe he felt it wouldn't work if he came in the door. These things are delicate. I did ask him to call in advance so I wouldn't have to be scared out of my shoes each time he visited, and he complied. Still it was a little scary because I couldn't be absolutely certain it was Ishmael at the window and not the Rapist because, after all, the Rapist didn't know anything about Ishmael's system and could as easily come on a night Ishmael called as one he didn't call.

Also I worried that Ishmael would want me to go through the whole routine each time: running to the window, screaming, crawling rapidly away up my nightgown, performing the swift, neat body-trundle under the bed.

But he didn't. All he asked was that I would be in bed when he arrived, come to the window when it went up, clasp him passionately in my arms when he came through. He would take it from there.

And my, how he did take it from there! It was always exciting.

One night, a particularly dark one, he came through the window naked and erect. What a surprise. When I clasped him in my arms we went right to it where we stood. By my wrapping one leg around the small of his back and standing tiptoe on the other, he was able to bend his knees a bit and successfully slip inside me. Then he put both hands under my buttocks and lifted me off the floor entirely. I wrapped my other leg around his waist. My arms, of course, were around his neck.

How, then, was one (or two, actually) to get the rhythmic motion going when combined this way? Well, that was the amazing thing. Holding me as described above, Ishmael moved me up and down, back and forth, round and round. And for a good long time too, a very good, very long, time. It was an amazing feat of upper-body strength. Well, leg strength too, I guess. It certainly warranted a letter to Doctors M. & J., I thought at the time, and do now. It was marvelous. It is hard to be orgasmic and astonished at the same time but, come to think of it, I succeeded. Ishmael did too. I was a little leery that when he came, he might forget himself and drop me, but he didn't.

By then he had maneuvered us closer to the bed and we both fell onto it, groaning our heads off. We lay in a hopeless, seemingly inextricable tangle for the longest time, trying to catch our breaths. "Water!" one of us cried. Probably me. My throat was terribly dry. "Water!" No, that was definitely Ishmael's voice. But getting water meant separating and I still couldn't tell whose limbs were whose.

"I'll get it," we both said.

"No, I'll get it. Let me."

We began to laugh. Our bodies shook with laughter. I felt him rise up in me again, rise up where he was, still inside me, rising hugely.

"No, no, stop. Please. I haven't the strength. Water!"

We laughed. We loved. Our hearts, united, beat with laughter, love, and lust. We rose and fell, dipped and rolled. The bed seemed luminous with love in the darkling room embedded in the darker night, Ishmael embedded in me. Laughing, murmuring nonsense that sustained the laughter, we swelled to another climax, an agonizingly sweet, shuddering one, and then, still all unwatered, we slept.

It was our nicest time together.

Which perhaps was too bad, because I didn't see him after that for about a week. Were nice times somehow threatening to Ishmael?

Another night he phoned to say he'd be by and after about forty-five minutes I heard the window go up but then, instead of him calling out, as I'd asked him always to do, "It's me, Ishmael," I heard another voice entirely.

The other voice said sternly, "What's going on here? What do you think you're doing? Just a minute now."

It was Mack.

I ran to the window and leaned out. Mack had Ishmael firmly by the arm. Brave Mack. Noble Mack. What a neighbor!

But poor Ishmael.

"I'm a friend of Ronda's," Ishmael was saying easily.

"You are? Well why don't you come in the door then?"

"It's all right," I said quickly. "He *is* my friend. Ishmael Scott, this is my neighbor, Mack Scher."

"Hi, Mack. I'm Joe. Call me Joe. Only Ronda calls me Ishmael."

"Oh, you're Joe Scott, the runner. I've seen you at races. I didn't know you were a friend of Ronda's."

"Do you want to come in, Mack?" I asked, still leaning out the window.

"Hell, no. I got work to do. I was just checking."

"Thanks a lot. I appreciate it. But Mack, wait!" He was walking away. I scrambled out the window and went after him. "I'll be right back," I said to Ishmael. "You go on in."

I caught up with Mack at the gate. It was a balmy evening with a gibbous moon. "Thanks for looking out for me, Mack. You had every right to be suspicious."

My nightgown was long-sleeved and demure but I crossed my arms over my bosoms. I'd never talked to Mack in a nightgown before. Nor had I stood outside in my yard in a nightgown before.

"Why doesn't he come in the door?" Mack asked.

I could lie to Mack and say that Ishmael usually did come in the door but then, if Mack saw him at the window again, which he undoubtedly would, he'd be bound to feel that he had to investigate again, and the whole scene would be endlessly reenacted. I was embarrassed, naturally, to explain the true situation. Very embarrassed.

"He just likes to come in the window," I said helplessly. "It's hard to explain."

Mack was silent and didn't look at me.

"But here's what I'm worried about now, Mack. I'm worried that sometime you might see the County Rapist at my window and not investigate because you'd just think it was Ishmael."

"Jee-sus!"

Mack just stood there, shaking his head.

"I'm serious," I said. It was important to impress him with my seriousness about this.

"I know you are. That's what worries me. Ronda, look, it's simple. Tell your friend Ishmael to use the door." He spoke slowly as if to a lip-reader. "Then, if I see a man at your window, I'll know it's the Rapist. Isn't that simple?"

"I don't think I can do that. It's hard to explain."

"You already said that."

It occurred to me that on the nights Ishmael called to

say he was coming, I could leave a note at Mack's to say that if there was a man at the window that evening, it would be Ishmael. But that seemed unduly elaborate and I really didn't want to involve Mack so deeply in my love life. There seemed no way out.

"Probably if you see anyone at my window from now on, you won't come and investigate," I said gloomily. "Right?"

"Right," Mack scowled. "Because the chances are about ninety-nine percent that it'll be your friend and I've got more important things to do than make an ass out of myself night after night."

"It isn't every night."

"Well, maybe you want to let me know the nights he's coming?"

"Could I?" I asked hopefully.

"No," said Mack, and walked across the street to his house.

"Jee-sus," I heard faintly, over the sound of his retreating steps.

I felt forlorn as I walked back to my house, dragging my heels. I felt I'd upset Mack. I knew he was upset and angry. I didn't like that. The other times when I'd done stupid things he seemed to be angry for me but not at me. I felt he was angry at me and it wasn't a good feeling. Well, not angry, but upset. I hadn't done anything to incur his anger, surely. I hadn't done anything at all, come to think of it—except create, or produce, rather, an odd... uh... circumstance, a bizarre sort of ...

Well, what *was* Mack so mad about?

When I got into the house and saw Ishmael lying naked on my bed, I forgot my unhappy feelings because he looked even more down in the mouth than me. Down in the genitals too.

"What's the matter, Ishmael?"

"It's not the same."

"What's not the same?"

"It's not the same when I come in the window just after you've gone out of it."

I laughed. "Yes, that must have been strange. It must have seemed sort of pointless. Poor Ishmael. Cheer up." While I was speaking, I was disrobing (disgowning), and now I lay down beside him but he wasn't cheering even a little way up. His "shaft," as he liked to call it, was lying doggo. I kissed him and caressed him, but nothing doing.

"Do you want to go outdoors and come in again?" I asked.

He considered it. "No, I don't think so."

"Did it discourage you having Mack try to apprehend you like that?" I wondered if it had plunged him into black memories of his doping days when cops were the constant enemy.

"No," he answered. "I didn't mind that. That's all right. That was nice of him—to look out for you."

"He's a good neighbor and a good friend. He's very dear to me."

I kissed Ishmael's nipples and sucked on them, which was something he enjoyed and it made me feel sexy, but he stayed limp as a fish. Musingly I stroked his penis. "It's the softest thing in the whole world. I mean even when it's hard, it's soft-feeling. The only think I can compare it to is a horse's muzzle. That wonderful, sensitive, silken softness."

"The inside of a woman is pretty special-feeling too."

"Is it?" I asked, pleased. I would have liked him to say more about it but he didn't. He was too gloomy to talk.

"All your skin is so beautifully textured," I went on. "So satiny. And I love your big veins." I traced them with my finger. "I love the big slow booming sound of your heart. What's your pulse rate? Around fifty?"

"Yes."

"I can hear your heart from a room away."

Silence—except for his heart.

"Shall I make some biscuits? How would you like some biscuits with butter and honey?"

"That's a great idea."

We had biscuits and some unbelievable strawberries and then Ishmael looked drowsy so I bundled him into bed and he spent the night for the first time and in the morning we woke up and made love just like any old married couple. He even gave a couple of token minutes to the missionary position before going into his elaborate combinations.

I felt perfectly willing, then, to change the modus operandi to making biscuits each time—arousal by biscuits— and do away with the entire window caper, but Ishmael was loath to give it up. He liked it. Just as long as I didn't go out the window before he came in. Which I promised never to do again.

During breakfast we had a little talk about his life. Tentatively I asked, "Do you still think of becoming a monk?"

"No. I'm getting more involved in writing lyrics now. The artist's life appeals to me. It's not so different from a monk's, really. A simple, pure, dedicated life. After I get some lyrics together, I want to try to sell them. Hook up with a singer, maybe. Or a group. All I'd need is one hit and I'd be set."

What naiveté, I thought sadly, motherly. Like the tyro story writer saying, all I need is one best-selling novel—not understanding that Nick the Greek is giving odds of one hundred thousand to one against. It would be a lot easier for Ishmael to make it as a monk—no competition.

But, as he talked on, I realized it wasn't the making it, or even the actual process of lyric writing, that called him; it was the life that seemed attractive, the life that, as I listened, revealed itself in face to be—my life.

My heart misgave me for Ishmael.

"I think you can't simply decide on a life, Ishmael. One's life evolves from one's work and being."

"Why not? Of course you can. You look around and say, 'That's the life for me!' "

"Yes, you say it, but you don't try to duplicate it. Because a life appears to be working well for one person, it doesn't follow that it might for you. It might really be antipathetical. I loved . . . this man. He was a truly talented person. He too thought he wanted to live the artist's life and came to live it here with me. He could not abide it, as it turned out. He deplored it. He ached for the life he had left. He was married to another woman at the time."

There, I'd finally said it. Now Ishmael knew all. Unconsciously I'd thrown my arm up as I spoke as if warding off a blow or, more likely, a religious tirade, but Ishmael didn't react at all, not so much as a flicker of an eyelid. Had he heard? I'd be damned if I was going to repeat it or spell it out in scarlet letters. He was self-absorbed. So I went back to the subject of his life.

"I don't know much about your life as you are living it now, Ishmael, since I've never seen your place. Tell me about it."

He grimaced.

"Please do. I like to be able to envision you when you are away from me."

"I live with some other people."

"A commune?"

"Not exactly. We're roommates. We share the rent. There are five of us; three women, two men. It's a mansion, actually."

"Oh? A mansion, Ishmael?"

Encouraged, he went on. "Yes. Hot tub, swimming pool, tennis courts . . . "

"Well for heaven's sake, I'm amazed, Stewardesses? Are your . . . your mansionmates stewardesses?"

"Yes. How did you know?"

"I see the classified ads. But I was quite taken in by that monk business," I said, and my mind was thinking, he probably has a washer, dryer, microwave oven, dishwasher,

TV, stereo, cleaning lady, pool-sweep, Japanese gardener. "Ishmael, I pictured you in a cell of some sort; I did."

"But it was true that I wanted to be a monk. It's just that it almost turns out to be cheaper to share a mansion than to rent a cell in this county."

I felt sad. I felt disappointed. I felt like a boob. In one fell swoop he had lost a lot of his romance for me. Underneath his hair shirt was Qiana.

But then, looking at Ishmael in all his beauty, with that interesting, lined forehead ennobling it, I knew I still felt moved by him in my heart, needed him in my loins. Even if he was a neurotic boy who didn't know what to do with himself. Even if the forehead was lined not by thought but by utter confusion, I had coupled my life to his. I cared about him. He was sensitive and nice, a fine athlete. He had kicked bad habits successfully, had purified his life considerably. That wasn't easy. I admired him for that and I would encourage him in any life he wanted to try.

In fact, how much better for him to be honestly confused than to be a religious nut who thought he had it all down pat.

He was saying, "Now I see that by writing inspired lyrics, I can serve God too, and live a godly life while doing it, a simple godly life, not austere, but simple: writing, running, a pure diet. I'm going to be a vegetarian now . . . "

I let him fantasize. I didn't ask him if he was going to go whole hog with purity and give up his mansion. I suppose you can live a simple godly life in a mansion as well as in a hermitage—all the modern-day Catholic hierarchy do.

Ishmael talked on, outlining his life, comparing it to the thoroughly evil lives all around him that revolved around greed, corruption, depravity, and meat-eating.

I began to wonder if after all Ishmael wasn't a religious nut who thought he had it all down pat.

5 . . .

A nother night—it was a Gramps' Night and we
were just bringing our bowls of soup out to the
picnic tables, which were no longer under the tent now that
it was spring—I thought I saw a figure disappear around
the corner of the back of the house. Gramps thought he did
too. "Hey! Who was that?"

"I saw him too!" said another.

They all struck up a chorus of exclamations. "Someone's sneaking around Ronda's house."

"It's a prowler!"

"Could be the Rapist!"

"Let's go get him."

Anxious to show off their newly acquired running
skills, they set down their soups and, to a man, including the
women, took off after my prowler with comparative alac-
rity. I hoped they wouldn't soon have a naked Ishmael at
bay. I'd told him always to call first, and he knew about
Mondays and Thursdays.

"You go that way." They divided up and went opposite
ways around the house, making good speed. I remained at
table where the glow of kerosene lanterns grew brighter in
the dusk and the vapors from the soups veiled the air.

Damned if they didn't catch him—the ones who went
"that way."

Breathless and excited, they brought him before me. It
was Joey Horgan, looking not at all discomfited.

There were some blacks among my company and one
man said, "What you think you doin', boy, messin' around
this fine woman's house?"

Joey grinned. "I'm just not sayin' nothin' till I get one of
them bowls of soup."

"I'd say you're too young for one of these old people's
bowls of soup," said another.

"Make him explain himself first," said Gramps.

But they were all feeling so inflated that they wanted to talk themselves, so they all ran on about how they'd caught Joey; then the others, who hadn't caught him, returned and told their stories and everyone sat down and spooned soup, so I quietly took Joey aside and told him, "Get the hell out of here."

"I just want to take some pictures of this here remarkable occasion."

"You are intruding."

But there was nothing I could do. Joey started snapping pictures and promised to give them all copies and they preened, some of them, or posed, or glared as the case may be, and all I could do was go in the house and not be in the pictures myself.

I was burned.

6 . . .

Maude was right about one thing. My feet got better. Thank heavens for that. After about two and a half weeks' layoff, I was able to start running again and I felt stronger than ever. Probably the enforced reprieve did my whole body a lot of good, by hastening its recuperation from the marathon. I had missed my running something fierce. I was glad to get back to my long, lone mountain runs, my race-pace flights with Ishmael, and sociable runs with Maude and Mack. So, for about a week my life seemed about as good as it could ever get—even with Blue and Moby gone—because I had wonderful runs, was working on an absorbing new story, doing interesting reading, saw no more of Joey Horagn, did not think once of Joe, or Louise, or the Rapist.

As well, the town and the mountain were radiant with spring. Every tree, shrub, and flower had burst all the barriers of bloom. For me, this was a time of grace. If Joey had been around, he would really have seen me glow. I couldn't put a step wrong. Every word I read I understood. When writing, my sentences sang, my paragraphs pulsed. Each day was bliss, was a dazzlement, and the days numbered a full week and then it ended.

Here's how it ended.

Feeling sick, Sam came home from San Diego like a wounded pet that will drag itself home over miles of terrain before licking its wounds and letting them heal. He'd been struck down by a terrible flu that was going around campus. It started with a sore throat and cough and then hit you with a high fever. Sam was just entering the fever phase when he walked in.

"Hi, Mom, I don't feel too good."

He'd called on the way so I was expecting him.

"Sam, you go to my bed and I'll sleep on the studio couch tonight. That way you can close the door and sleep and not be disturbed by my typing or by anything. Poor Sam. You look ghastly."

"Pretty much—sick as a dog."

I took his temperature and it was a hundred and three. I gave him aspirins and forced him to drink a lot of juice and water. Finally I made him some hot bouillon from my stock pot, which I served him in bed. He conked out. I decided not to write and did quiet chores instead, washed out some bits of wardrobe and hung them out to dry, washed and waxed the kitchen floor. It is good to do mindless chores when feeling concerned.

Four hours later I heard movement in the bedroom so I looked in. Sam was up and dressed. He brushed by me, going hell for leather out the door. I grabbed him.

"Where on earth do you think you're going?"

"What?"

He was delirious, didn't know what he was doing. Luckily he was manageable. I laid him down on the bed and took his temperature. It was a hundred and four! I was terrified. I stripped off all his clothes, got him on his feet again, into the bathroom and under a cold shower. I toweled him dry, then put him in bed naked, with just a sheet over him. His temperature, thank God, had withdrawn to one hundred and two. Compliantly he took more aspirins, drank juices. He fell asleep again.

Now it was night. I hovered by his bed. He would be all right. All Sam's life, I mused, he had gotten sick like this: suddenly, violently, briefly. He'd never spent more than a day in bed, but what a day that would always be. Tummy flu—the vomit would fly. Fevers—always like this. Colds—a totally clogged head, streaming eyes and nose, no voice. He condensed a week-long sickness into one day to get it done with so he could be off and running again.

I thought about the little spider monkey he was when a baby, five percent body fat even then. Other mothers felt sorry for me. He had milk-white skin and everywhere a filigree of veins. Blue veins all over his head instead of hair. Yes, other mothers would cluck their tongues and say what a shame he didn't look like a "normal" baby, chubby and sweet—but I had the last cluck when he was up on his feet at six months and really putting them to use at seven, uncatchable at eight. While their babies were still lying there drooling—being chubby and sweet.

And how he loved the breast. He'd scream for it, and my milk, answering, would come streaming out even while I was two rooms away. I'd laugh to give him the nipple and hear the mighty, lusty, sound cut off in mid-scream as he clamped his avid mouth to it to guzzle the sweet milk down. He would never hold my breast. His little hands would whirl through the air as he sucked, some ecstatic wrist motion that whirled his hands like pinwheels as he sucked.

I wondered if he didn't find himself wanting to do that nowadays during the ecstasy of love, trying to figure how on earth to arrange a minute with both hands free and still keep everything going. I smiled. He'd manage. My Sam could do anything.

I decided I'd better not sleep that night in case Sam took it in his head to go wandering again. I made myself supper—a nice green salad with a scattering of baby shrimps—and set a small fire just for the comfort and color because it was a warm, pleasant night. I lay on the rock-hard studio couch and delved into Singer's book *Shosha*.

Ishmael called and I told him all about Sam. He commiserated. We talked a little, said good-bye. I threw some more logs on the fire and read on. The minutes ticked along. Periodically I looked in on Sam. At the proper time I woke him up enough to give him aspirins again. He gabbled all sorts of nonsense in his sleep. Time passed. Maybe I drowsed a little, but only a little because I clearly heard the bedroom window when it went up.

I didn't react at once. That's weird, I thought. I certainly made it clear to Ishmael not to come tonight. Perhaps I didn't actually *say* not to come but I said that Sam was here sick, was in my bed sick . . . Did I say he was in my bed? Even if I didn't, it isn't very thoughtful of Ishmael. It's quite bad of him actually. I do wonder about Ishmael sometimes. Really!

Feeling extremely annoyed, I got up, unwound myself from the afghan I must have put over me at some point, and went to the bedroom. I'd left the door ajar. I quietly swung it wide, looked in. As I did so, I heard a strange gasp. I saw, not Ishmael, but some unknown person, dressed all in black, standing over Sam where he lay on the bed with the sheet thrown back.

The inevitable had happened. The Rapist had come. It was almost as if my fear had conjured him up, that my obsession had created his coming. And how like life to play its eternal trick of catching me sleeping or, rather, lulling me to sleep, so as to catch me all unawares and unsuspecting. Just when I had let down my surveillance, put the

Rapist out of my mind for an entire week, he elected to come.

I did not flee, scream, or in any way quail. On the contrary, I greeted his appearance with a glad heart. At last! was my first thought. What a relief to finally confront the accursed, feared thing rather than continue to live with it hovering around the edges of my life and consciousness like an incurable illness, like the cancer that had tried to lodge in me, not causing any pain but making me play host to it, eating away at me, malign and vile, eating me out of house and home.

At last!

Now I would go forward and do battle with this thing. It was not only the necessary and inevitable confrontation with the evil in my life but it was me being the lioness protecting her cub. The villain was at the bed of my helpless boy.

Undoubtedly, seeing the long blond hair and soft cheek against the pillow, he had been flabbergasted to remove the sheet and find fine male genitals draped against Sam's slender loins. I would catch him at this moment of stupefying astonishment.

Brother Rapist, I pray you be courteous with me, I muttered to myself, a hasty litany. Then, not at all in the spirit of St. Francis, I launched myself through the air and hit Brother Rapist with a flying tackle. The lamp fell to the floor with a crash. Sam came to. "Wha . . . ?"

"Call Mack, Sam. Call him or run for him. Get him over here. Quick!"

Sam moved. Groggily, but he moved.

I was rolling around the floor with the Rapist, punching him whenever and wherever I could but apparently not doing him any serious harm to judge by his vigor. Imagine my astonishment—his own of a moment ago was as nothing—when I felt breasts. I stopped rolling and lay aghast as I felt his female breasts. Big ones too.

7 . . .

*I*n short, it was Louise Masterson. And she categorically denied that she was the Rapist.

Mack's face was a study when he walked in and saw me and Louise getting up off the bedroom floor.

Sam crawled back into bed and conked out.

"This woman has attacked me," said Louise, right off the bat, without blinking an eye.

But I doubt that Mack heard her say that because I was loudly crowing, "I've got her. I've got the Rapist, Mack. It's her."

"This woman is crazy," said Louise.

"Arrest her, Mack. She's the Rapist. I know it's unbelievable. I'm staggered myself. But it's true. Louise Masterson is the County Rapist. Book her!"

"I've never heard anything so ridiculous and outrageous," she responded acidly.

Sam groaned.

"Let's go into the living room," said Mack, about-facing. We followed him out of the bedroom. "Okay, sit down, please."

I remained standing but Louise sat on the couch with its tangle of afghan. In the lamplight I could see she was dressed in a chic black jumpsuit. Her short, dark, curly hair was not disheveled from our tussle but her face was a little rearranged.

In the fireplace, coals still burned brightly.

"Let's get this ironed out," Mack said. "First of all, is everybody okay?"

"I'd like some ice for my eye," said Louise.

"Ronda, looks like you gave her a black eye. Got any ice?"

"What? No. The heck with her eye. She can call an ophthalmologist if she wants. Listen, Mack. She came into my bedroom through the window. She didn't have the least idea this was my house. Sam was in my bed because he's sick. She just about had a cardiac arrest when she pulled back the sheet and saw it was a man ... "

"She's lying," said Louise, cool as any cucumber.

"What?" I quacked again. Every time she or Mack spoke I was confounded. It was as if they were at another occasion entirely. "Me lying? But it's plain as day. You're here, aren't you? You're dressed in black. Probably there's a knife somewhere in the bedroom. And rope. You must be so surprised it's me. It sure is a night of surprises for you, Louise. For me too, I must admit. But especially for you. It's not easy to be a rapist these days. So many unknowns."

I was walking up and down the small bare room, gesticulating, overexcited I admit, but who wouldn't be? Now I paused to look triumphantly at Mack. "Go ahead and arrest her, Mack. I bet you get a citation."

"Hold on just a minute ... "

"Hold on for what?"

"I'd like to hear what Mrs. Masterson has to say about all this."

"Okay, but you better tell her her rights first. Read her her rights. Admonish her. Reel off the old Miranda."

Mack ignored me. "Mrs. Masterson?" he said politely.

"This woman has been harassing me for several months. I'd finally had enough. I decided to come down here and have it out with her."

"In the middle of the night?" I squealed.

"It's nine forty-five right now," said Mack.

"It is?"

"I thought if I could talk with her in a civilized manner," Louise went on, "then maybe she'd see reason. I can see now that was an absurd hope. The woman is mad as a hatter."

My jaw dropped. The unmitigated gall of her. The temerariousness! I was ready to spring at her throat but I contained myself. The time had come, I saw, to contain myself. A little yogic breathing was indicated here. Why did I never get a mantra like everybody else?

Trying to duplicate her detached ironic tone, I asked, "And if one has come for a civilized talk, does one enter through the window, the bedroom window? Does the hell one?"

"I entered through the front door," she told Mack, "which was open,"

I saw now that she was formidable. I, who have a complete inability to lie, was out of my league here. Every lie she uttered absolutely knocked the breath out of me.

"The door was open when I came," said Mack.

"Of course it was. Sam had just gone out of it to get you."

"Oh, that's right," said Mack, looking a little embarrassed.

"Let's ask Sam if it was open when he went out," Louise suggested.

We went into the bedroom and turned on the light. The lamp was still on the floor, books had tumbled from the shelf, everything had spilled from Sam's pack. In response to our question Sam said, "Graagh. Sunday's good but February's better. This is damned fun," rolling over a few times as he spoke.

"Sam's sick as a dog," I said, leading the way back into the living room. "He's no help as a witness. He's been out of it all night. But Mack, you believe me. Of course you believe me." With a sudden chill I saw that possibly he didn't. "It's me, Ronda, your best friend. You know I don't lie, Mack."

"To continue with my story, Sergeant," said Louise, sitting down again and actually folding the afghan into a neat square as she talked—and there was nothing in the whole world that could have made her seem less like a rapist than that one act—"as you know very well, *as the whole town can tell you,* this woman has been a thorn.

"It began several months ago when she heaved a rock through my window one night. Since then there has been a series of annoyances perpetrated by her, including phone calls to my house, culminating in her throwing a flower pot at me."

Every good liar knows how to use as much truth as possible and that was what she was doing. Wisely, I kept silent. I was not going to be thrown on the defense. I sat down on the floor, arranging myself in the lotus position. It was for her to defend herself. She was the accused, not me, although I was beginning to look awfully accused. Pretty much—accused, as Sam would say. Somehow I couldn't get around the feeling that it was me in the dock, not her. How this was happening I couldn't figure out. I was even beginning to sweat. Ever since Mack had entered, she had been the impressive one. It was lucky that Mack knew me. What if it had been a strange policeman hearing all this?

Or *was* it lucky that Mack knew me?

Louise finished her little speech for the prosecution, " . . . so I came to try to talk reason to her and she attacked me."

"Why were you in the bedroom, Louise?" I asked her calmly. "Inquire of her why she was in the bedroom, Mack."

"I entered this house through the open door. It is a curious arrangement she has here. She has turned the entrance hall into a little workroom of some sort . . . "

"It's my writing room!"

"And then one comes to the kitchen, which has two doors off it: one to the bedroom and one to the living room and how was I to know which was which? I saw her car outside so I knew she was here. I went through the first door, which turned out to be the bedroom. I hesitated but decided that since I'd come this far I might as well see her even if it meant waking her up. It wasn't an easy mission to begin with, Sergeant, as you can imagine. You probably know the whole story."

I leaped up. I sprang to my feet, which is very hard to do from the lotus position. "Let's go back to the bedroom. You'll see that the window is wide open."

We went back to the bedroom and the window was closed. "But . . . " My mind ranged furiously. "Sam must have closed it. Or maybe the sound I heard was her *shutting* the window after she'd come through it."

"Probably she was asleep in the living room when I arrived and has since dreamed up all this window business," said Louise pityingly.

It enraged me the way she talked of me to Mack in the third person as if I weren't in the room. It made me want to look around for myself. "She was not asleep," I said. "She was wide awake reading *Shosha*," I said to Louise, "and she is getting more and more pissed off with your bald-faced lies."

There was plenty of light in the bedroom now from the full moon low in the sky outside, and joyfully I saw on the floor, half under the bed, "The knife!" I grabbed for it and displayed it to Mack. "Proof positive. We need say no more. Take her away."

"It is not my knife," she said. "I never saw that knife before in my life."

She said it with such self-possession, such certainty, that I actually gave the knife a keen look to see if it was by any chance mine. The woman was an absolute master of prevarication.

"May I go now, Sergeant? I am feeling a little anxious about my eye."

"Sure, go on. Sorry about all this."

"Mack!"

"Hold on. I'll be right back to talk to you. I'll just see Mrs. Masterson to her car."

"Where is her car? I'll be interested to see if she has a car parked outside."

She did. A white Mercedes. Parked right outside my gate. I went back inside and paced about in a mounting rage.

"Mrs. Masterson," I muttered through my teeth, "Mrs. Masterson," I snarled at Mack when he came in. "Why didn't you call her Mayoress Masterson? Or your majesty, while you were at it?"

"I had nothing to hold her on, Ronda. I couldn't prove breaking and entering. Assault? She was the one with the shiner. Rape? No way. Nobody's been raped here tonight. I have to have probable cause. There is no way I could break her story, and to be honest I'm inclined to believe her story. I think it's possible that she wanted to talk to you, came down, walked in, you were asleep, et cetera, et cetera. I don't think you're a reliable witness in this instance. If Sam didn't happen to be delirious, of course I'd believe anything he had to say, but as it is . . ." Mack spread his hands. "You can see my position."

I wrung my hands. "I could weep, Mack. I could weep. That you would believe her over me . . . "

"I believe you, Ronda. I know you're not lying. But it's a matter of what you perceive to be true. Everything you tell me is what you think, not what you know. I have to keep to the facts and the facts are . . . "

"But it all fits. Doesn't it all fit when you think about it? I happen to know she's a cold woman, frigid, hates sex with a man . . . "

"Do you know that for a fact? How could you possibly know that for a fact? At the most you'd know it on hearsay. And all married men tell their mistresses their wives are cold."

"They do? Really? But . . . but I believe Joe because he didn't really say it in so many words . . . I . . . "

It really threw me, Mack saying that about married men. But I took heart and went on with postulating my proofs. "And there's the fellatio angle, Mack. What about that?"

"The what?"

"The fact that the Rapist likes oral sex and never has entered his victims. That means the Rapist could be a woman, right?"

"Cunnilingus. I think you mean the cunnilingus angle."
"Oh."

We both laughed. A release from tension. When I recovered, I said, "Both those words are unbelievable. I can't imagine where they came from. They're chimerical. As if they were the names of some fabled beasts. The cunnilingus would be a sort of waddling, armadillolike creature with an excessive amount of multicolored toes," I walked about imitating a cunnilingus, "and the fellatio would be a flying animal, like the pterodactyl of yore . . . " I flapped my arms vigorously.

"Okay if I have a beer?" Mack went to the fridge.

"I wish Maude were here to make me a tea with rum," I said woefully. "That's what she gives me at trying times in my life. And I'm truly tried tonight. Truly and sorely."

"Put the kettle on. I'll be right back with some rum."

I put the kettle on and checked in on Sam. He was sleeping easily and felt cooler.

In the kitchen again, I looked at the knife. Now that I had stupidly got fingerprints on it, she could always say hers had got on while grabbing it from me when I attacked her. Still, it wouldn't hurt at all to have Mack "dust it." This was my only "fact." It was one of those good sharp wooden-handled kitchen knives with a steel blade, not stainless. It was the kind I used myself. But it was not mine. I did not have one that size.

When Mack returned, he set down the pint of Bacardi, wrapped up the knife, and put it in a plastic bag without my even asking him to. I felt comforted. What a good cop.

I steeped a Sleepytime teabag in a mug of water, added lemon and rum. "Just for the record, Mack, I did not throw a rock through the Mastersons' window. The weird thing is that I actually considered doing it, but I couldn't think of a good note to attach to it, so I didn't. These things matter a lot to a writer."

"You've got to admit, just for the record, that you've

done a few malicious things I know about and it follows that you've probably done at least as many I don't know about."

"But that's the funny thing. I haven't. You know them all. You're such a damned ubiquitous cop."

"What about the phone calls?"

"One. One phone call. That's all. There was something I wanted to tell Joe. Well, two." I blushed. "I had to call him back . . . " Three, I thought to myself. But that one was a call to the bank.

"I know you don't lie. But I think sometimes you don't remember."

In the living room I stirred up the fire and Mack and I sat down on the studio couch. I wanted to talk more about the evening. I wanted to say a million things. But I didn't. I felt empty-headed. I couldn't think of anything to say. There'd been too much talk already, too many lies. Silence was so pure, so truthful.

I sipped my tea and let the warmth flow through me; the warmth of fire and tea and friendship. Drink deep, benefits reap. How did it go? I couldn't remember.

"When I was doing research on camels for a story recently, I learned that despite their distinguished, benignant appearance, they are stupid, recalcitrant, obnoxious, untrustworthy, and openly vicious. I'd say that's a perfect description of Louise."

"I just never did hear of a woman rapist," was the only thing Mack had to say. "Homosexual rape, yes. Men, though. It just doesn't make sense, Ronda. What does make sense though is that she might have come here with the intent to harm you. That's something to think about, something to seriously consider—that she might have wanted to harm you."

"She's the County Rapist, Mack. You'll see."

When Mack left, I wanted so much to call Ishmael and ask him to come over and give me some nice hugs. Just some nice warm hugs was all I wanted. But that was the sort of thing Ishmael couldn't do. It was too simple. He was not an affectionate person. He was not a warm person. Anyhow, I didn't know his number.

After my hot rum I took a turn around the house. I didn't leave my yard for fear of wandering into someone else's. I didn't have Blue anymore to help me home.

8 . . .

*T*he next day I went into my "little work room of some sort" (Grrr!), sat down at my desk, and had the feeling that I was up against a wall, head on. Lactic acid buildup of the brain.

I believe that I am responsible for myself, that whatever happens, good or bad, there is no one else to blame or reward. I try to have no expectations of other people or of the unknowable future.

I fell away from this with Joe—put faith in him, let expectations flourish, visualized a future. I guess that is the nature of love but it shouldn't be. I should have learned that from my marriage with Alan.

One day, on a trail, a rock somehow came undone from its place in the ground where it had lodged for who knows how many years and, because of a downward slope, it began to move, first over earth and then through air. It gained momentum and, although not large, its mass combined with its velocity to give it enough strength and weight to easily bash in a human skull. And, although it finally could have come to rest anywhere on miles of possible ground, it hit Alan instead and our future was snuffed out with his life. I kissed him good-bye that morning and, against all expectations, he never came home again.

But . . . what was I saying?

Oh yes, I should have learned from that. But I gave my all to Joe, nevertheless, gave all I own in air from the red-woods softly blown.

However, I let him go gracefully. Did you notice? No scenes. When he gave me the word, that was that. Good-bye, I said. Don't call me. And I never blamed him. I suffered but I handled it pretty well—except for the episode of the tires and the couple of phone calls, I handled it and tried to figure it out and learn from it. (And the Geranium Incident. I keep forgetting that. Damn. That was bad. That wasn't a good one. And the pinch? I still don't know whether to count the pinch.)

Taped to my desk for many years, much doodled on by Sam, are some of Chekhov's words from a letter to his friend.

> My holy of holies is the human body, health, intelligence, talent, inspiration, love, and the most absolute freedom—freedom from violence and lying, whatever forms they take. This is the program I would follow if I were a great artist.

It seemed to me I had gotten away from the program because violence had come into my life. I felt threatened from every side. Violence and lying too. Oh, a lie is a terrible thing.

It was terrifying to feel that the events of my life were out of control, being moved by some relentless force that was not a good force but a power of evil. This feeling of loss of freedom was a vision of the abyss opening, widening, deepening at my feet. And the ground moving under me, nothing to hold onto, no support, no handhold, no sense of myself. The ground trembling, me trembling, oh why couldn't my skin be still? I was so tired of trembling, shivering, shuddering ...

If I could talk it out with Maude and have her bring the clear, cold light of her intelligence to the situation, mightn't that help? No, it would still be mere speculation. I saw that what I must do was talk to Joe, talk to Joe about Louise.

Accordingly I put my hand on the phone—my trembling hand.

But where to meet? We could not meet here because of Sam. We could not meet at a public place because of gossip. Certainly we could not meet at his house.

The mountain!

I called the bank. "He's in conference," said his secretary.

"I, too, wish to confer with him," I said. "Please tell him to meet me at the junction of the Hukuiku and Matt Davis trails at five this evening." I impressed her with the imperative nature of our conference. "Nothing must stand in the way of his coming."

"Okay, Ronda." She was a woman I trusted, "Okay, kid," she said.

I couldn't do any writing so I went into the bedroom to visit with Sam, who was much improved but still weak, and taking it easy.

"The dreams I had!" he said. "Did I walk in my sleep?"

"You were up and around a bit. Kept me on my toes all right."

"I seem to remember going outside, to Mack's. Or did I dream that? How come you didn't stop me? Seems like you *told* me to go to Mack's. What was going on here last night anyway?"

"Un . . . well . . . hmmm."

There was no sense in confiding any of it to Sam. If he could remember anything and be helpful, I would. Then I'd happily unload the whole affair. I never kept much from Sam. But as it was . . .

"Did the Rapist finally come?" He laughed. It struck him as excessively funny. To say I was unamused is an understatement. Nor need I say how bitterly I was thinking that only a boy or man could find the subject a mirthful one.

"Pretty much—not amused," said Sam.

"Damn right."

"You're losing your sense of humor."

"That's not all I'm losing."

Sam hoisted himself up higher in bed. "Let's see who can dial our telephone number the fastest." He got out his stopwatch. With the receiver on we took turns dialing, being timed by the other person. It was exciting. After a while at this sporting event, I held the record at 0:7:33. Sam couldn't break 0:7:39. It cheered me up. Nothing like winning something (even this!) to feel a little bit back in control.

"Now the left hand," said Sam.

Sam's 0:7:93 won it for the left hand. I couldn't break 0:7:97.

"Pinkies?"

"I draw the line at pinkies. Timed-left-hand-home-number-dialing is the bottom line on time wasting. If we go to pinkies, it will be noses next."

I got off the bed, "When are you due to appear at your Youth Conservation Corps job?"

"Tomorrow."

"No! So soon!"

"If I hadn't got sick I would probably have just gone straight up to Oregon from college."

"And you won't be back until August," I mourned.

"But then I'll have more than a month until school starts."

I felt his forehead for fever. "I have to meet someone now. I'll be back at seven and make you a nice farewell dinner. Steak?"

"Face!"

9 . . .

O utside, on the lane, as I prepared to get into the Honda, I saw a running figure round the corner.

Why, that's Ishmael, I thought. I wonder why he didn't stop in to say hello. Maybe he's shy because Sam's here. But how queer for him to be running through this part of town. He always runs on the mountain or out to the ocean. Maybe it wasn't Ishmael.

I got in the car. Then, as I started the engine, I forgot about Ishmael because, through the windshield I saw, rounding the corner at the other end of the lane—Joey Horgan!

I felt like the Lone Ranger when he was encircled by Indians: "Tonto, we're surrounded."

"What do you mean *we*, white man?"

Like the L.R., I felt both surrounded and abandoned.

I took the first right and headed up the mountain to meet Joe.

Utterly Raped

1 . . .

Joe arrived at the junction of trails exactly on time.
It was a fine afternoon on the mountain. Wild
lilac bushes bordered the trails in clouds of astonishing blue
while the shy wild iris skulked among the ground cover,
more exquisite than any orchid, fragile and ephemeral-
seeming against the drop of redwood trees that towered to
the sky in a mighty mountain regiment of the tallest trees on
earth.

I had on my yellow dolphin shorts and my gold Heart
of the Empire 15-Kilo shirt—a good-luck outfit.

I saw Joe coming with his long loose stride and I waved,
but when he got to me we stood awkwardly, not knowing
how to greet each other. I found it hard to look at him and I
turned away, gesturing to the Hukuiku. "Shall we walk as we
talk?"

"No, let's go down to the creek and sit."

We clambered off the trail, down over the rocky
ground to the creek, and sat on the needled bank. Now that
I did look at him I thought he looked angry. It was the angry
look he got when he was upset and trying not to show it. He
fixed a burning blue gaze on me, dry ice.

"How's Louise's eye?" I asked and, in spite of myself, a
giggle escaped me, probably a nervous giggle.

"Not very well."

"Maybe that will keep her home nights."

"I took her to the hospital this morning. She has a broken nose."

I did not express dismay, not feeling any. Nor did I reveal that I was tickled pink.

What I wanted to do was go directly to the heart of the matter of this meeting, but getting there was tricky.

How do you tell your ex-lover you think his wife is the County Rapist?

"You seem to have come out unscathed," he said, "which is remarkable considering that Louise has half a foot and forty pounds on you. But then," he added dryly, "you've always had supernatural powers."

"We saints do," I said. "There's pretty strong evidence around that I'm a saint."

"There's even stronger evidence that you're a lunatic."

"There's a fine line between the two. It's a line that fascinates me. I don't want to be either one, though. I just want to be the lone juice drinker. Instead I am beset by difficulties and . . . rapists." I added rapists because it seemed like a good lead-in to the subject I wished to arrive at.

But he picked up on . . . "The lone juice drinker?" looking bewildered. Gone was the icy glare. "What's that?"

"It's the me I aspire to be—free, independent, unabashed. But to return to my tussle with Louise. You understand that our fight took place in the dark. I didn't know it was her at the time. I don't want you to think we were . . . fighting over you."

"In the dark?"

"Joe, have you heard about the County Rapist?"

"Of course. It's a terrible thing. It's hard to believe that any man could do that. It must be a rare man who . . ."

"I know. And in fact it's my belief that it's not a man, it's a woman."

"How on earth . . .?"

"It's Louise."

"Ronda," he creased his brow with concern and took my hand.

I removed my hand from his. I went through the whole story. I told him all the facts of what was known about the Rapist and what had transpired last night regarding window, black clothes, knife, Sam's genitals, gasps, lies—the works.

"Ronda. I agree with you that Louise had no right to come to your house last night without warning. There you were, worried about Sam . . ."

"Joe, don't try to protect her. She's a sick woman. She's a dangerous woman. She is terrorizing this whole county!"

"Ronda, the Rapist is a black man."

"Louise is as big as a man. She has curly black hair. She's frigid . . ."

"Louise is not frigid."

"You said she was."

"I never said that."

"I believed it to be true. You gave me to believe . . ." I faltered. It hurt me to hear that. If indeed she had been willing to give him warm physical love, why had he come to me? Was he in fact sleeping with her as well, those months when we were lovers, maybe even when we were living together? What does it matter now—if it even mattered then? What matters now, I told myself, is not my personal feelings but the fact that my whole Rapist theory had to collapse under this new knowledge, for the whole theory was built on the foundation that Louise was a repressed lesbian who, as the first lady of the town, couldn't exercise her true sexuality and was driven to dressing as a man and seizing her perverse satisfaction from frail, frightened women of the county.

"Well," I said weakly, "if it is not true, then last night becomes even more of a mystery. I cannot understand her behavior. And the knife? What of the knife? Of course she denies it's hers, but it isn't mine, Joe. Joe, your sympathies seem to be with Louise and her broken nose, but I beg you to throw some light if you can on what occurred with us last night."

Joe was quiet. He'd picked up a handful of pebbles and was tossing them into the creek water.

"She is jealous of you, Ronda."

"Why?" I squealed. "What on earth has she to be jealous of now? It's been seven months since you went back to her and we've never met since, until today. There's nothing to be jealous *about*."

"A woman knows."

"Knows! There's nothing to know."

"I don't have to do anything or say anything but she still knows that . . . I love you."

I flushed and scrambled to my feet. "You have no right to say that. No right. It isn't fair."

"It's nevertheless true."

"I'm going. I'm not staying to talk to you any further. That was a terrible thing for you to say. You killed our love, Joe. You dealt it the death blow and now you say you still love me as if nothing destructive had happened."

He, too, got to his feet. He held out his arms to me. "I never said I stopped loving you."

Oh to enter those arms and lay my head on that dear breast. What surcease from trouble. What nepenthe. The end of loneliness. Of fear.

And then? More pain probably. And the work of months come all undone. No. He ought not to spread his arms like that. I backed away. "No. I've worked and worked to heal myself and all this time you've done nothing. Nothing! Just blithely gone on loving me as if nothing had happened. As if . . ."

He dropped his arms.

"You asked me to explain Louise to you. I have. You begged me to clear up the mystery. So I did. Listen to me, then. Louise is torn up with jealousy. She hates the very sight of you. She has me back but only the shell of me.

She knows I still belong to you and it's tearing her up."

"Well, don't do that to her. Tell her you'll try to love her. You should. You went back to her. What's the point of going back if you're not going to work at the marriage, create something good of it? As it is, it sounds worse than it was before we met. It's rotten, sickening. It's no way for either of you to live. Ugh! A beautiful house with all that going on behind its walls. What's the matter with people? Why do they do the things they do?"

"I had to go back to her. She needed me. She was desperately unhappy, had gone into a decline, was deeply depressed, unable to cope. What could I do? What was the decent thing to do?"

"You don't live with someone out of pity, feeding their dependency. That's no kindness to them. She'd have come out of her depression in time and begun to make a life for herself exclusive of you. I did."

"You're strong."

"I have no one hanging around keeping me weak. And in the end, Joe, the slave becomes the master. The weak one wields the power because they want more of you and more and more, even to the little spark of love left in your heart for me."

"It's not a little spark."

I had a vision of just how big the flame was—just enough to light up, on a dark night, the inside of a privy, to take a shit by.

Not a nice vision. I didn't give it utterance. As long as the saint-lunatic controversy still raged, I might as well give sainthood the edge.

I regained the trail, saying, "I'm going now, Joe. I'll return by the Hukuiku and you can take the Matt Davis. You'll be gone from the parking lot by the time I get there and no one will know we met. No one will see us together and bruit it about the town. You can relax on that score."

"Ronda. Don't go. You sound so bitter. This whole

meeting has gone wrong. I want to talk to you. I want to help you. I feel responsible for what's happening. Please!"

"Good-bye."

I began to run along the trail. I ran four miles in twenty-five minutes. Then I went into the Mountain High for a long lone deep drink of boysenberry apple.

2 . . .

C alifornia's idea of Virginia Woolf sat at the bar of the Mountain High wondering how to proceed.

What it all seemed to come down to was that Louise hadn't come to rape me, only to kill me.

Now, I totted up, there was someone who wanted to rape me and someone who wanted to kill me, and there was Joey Horgan who wanted to take me.

I felt beset.

Why was I so sure the Rapist was after me? I don't know. All fears are unreasonable. But if it is customary for a person to fear a snake or a cat or a height, why can't it obtain that one can fear a rapist? Especially when it's a known fact that one is prowling your own town and having a great success. It doesn't seem in the least an unreasonable fear, looked at like that.

In fact, I was more afraid of the Rapist than of Louise. Because I could understand Louise.

Even with my "rape readings," I still couldn't understand rape. Whenever I brought up the subject to man or woman, a look of horror and incomprehension sprang to their eyes. Rape is a horrible and incomprehensible act.

Who wouldn't be afraid? And certainly there'd been a lot of action at my bedroom window to fuel my fears.

If only Moby would come through my window.

If only something nice would happen.

I felt very low. I felt already raped. I felt as I imagine one would feel during the aftermath of rape. Used up. What was it the rape lecturer said? Internally destroyed. That was it. Internally destroyed and utterly powerless. But there was no sense in rehashing all the feelings I felt at the writing table earlier—the abyss and all that.

I sighed, left a dollar for my juice, and went out of the Mountain High up to the lot, into my Honda, and down to the town.

The main thing was to try to be cheerful for Sam's last night. Then I would try to begin life again tomorrow, try to learn to live it again. Tomorrow I would wave Sam away to the Tule Lake Fish and Game Preserve in Klamath Falls, Oregon. Another fleeting visit. That's how it would be for the rest of my life, fleeting visits from Sam.

In town I bought steak, mushrooms, potatoes, and petit pois to make Sam his favorite meal.

Maybe, I thought, as I got out of the Honda with my marketing, I'll invite Mack over for dinner. Sam would like that and I would too.

I set the shopping bag inside the gate and went down to Mack's, where I saw his door was open.

I stopped before I reached it, hearing a female voice. If he had a lady friend there it would be tactless to burst in and invite him to dinner.

The female voice was saying, "That's weird of Ronda. That doesn't sound good to me at all." It was Maude.

"Nothing sounds good," she went on in response to an agreeing grunt from Mack. "I'm really worried about her."

I remained and listened. I hunkered down by the door and listened with all my might. I spied.

Naturally I was curious to know what was "weird of Ronda." So I spied, an old device of storytellers.

They were silent now. I heard a chopping sound, knife on bread board.

"It's very disturbing," said Maude.

"Yeah," said Mack.

I began to fume. This conversation wasn't moving the story forward at all. It was too oblique. What was disturbing? What weird?

"And she's so thin."

Thin! Of course I'm thin. Lean and mean we call it in the running subculture.

"I think that marathon really took it out of her."

"That and Blue dying, Moby going," Mack's voice, "the cancer scare."

Cancer scare! Maude had no right to tell Mack about that. This obviously wasn't the first conversation between them re: Ronda.

"She's very sensitive," said Mack. "An artist, you know. A sensitive artist. Artists are different. They live different than other people and what happens to them in life, they handle different."

I preened. That was me all right. A sensitive artist. I preened but I also felt suddenly, strangely weepy. It was touching, what Mack had said. It was tender. It moved me. My eyes and nose filled.

You can't spy and snuffle at the same time. I invoked yogic disciplines to maintain my silence and stillness, letting my nose run. But thirty-five years of training told me that a lady, in any situation, does not allow snot on her face. I had loosened up a lot on this score during my running years. I thought nothing of wiping my nose on my sleeve or cavalierly blowing out a nostril into the air in the same spirit of letting fly a tongueful of spit.

But that's different from sitting quietly and letting it run down your face.

There were more chopping sounds. Mack just loved to chop up vegetables.

I decided to stand up, wipe my nose on my shirttail, and make my entrance.

All of which I did, saying, "Hi, Mack. Hi Maude." Then I stopped, stunned. The instrument behind all this chopping noise was Louise's knife! The only clue! The fact!

"Mack, that's the knife! That should be down at the laboratory, not here in your kitchen. Or did you test it already?"

"Aw, Ronda, I just took it away to please you. There's no way I could've gotten prints off that wooden handle, especially after you'd handled it. You need a smooth, hard, shiny surface to get good prints. And even if I did get some off it, how am I going to ask Mrs. Masterson to give us a pair of prints to compare them with?"

Maude stood up and took my hand. "Miss, I really don't think Louise is the County Rapist."

"I know. I've already been disabused of that notion. It doesn't hang together anymore. But it is nevertheless true that she came into my house with a knife last night—that knife," I pointed, "and I'd like to be believed about it."

"Well, that's a relief."

"What is?"

"That you don't think she's the Rapist."

Maude and Mack did look enormously relieved. They smiled at each other. They enjoyed an absolute festival of relief. I guess that had been what was "weird of Ronda," my thinking that Louise was the rapist.

Was it weird?

It had made perfect sense last night.

I didn't feel this great relief everyone was enjoying.

"Did you hear what I just said about the knife? Louise was there, right? I didn't invite her down. She came in the middle of the night with a knife, through the bedroom window. Do you find that at all alarming? How do I know that she's not in back of everything? Maybe she poisoned Blue and stole my cat."

Their relieved smiles were fast disappearing. Maybe, I thought, but didn't say, Louise forged a pap smear report, altered the one from the lab. Why not? Anything's possible in this world. Anything! Especially if you are consumed by jealousy, which Joe maintains she is. If you are an obsessed person you'll stop at nothing.

But I didn't suggest all this to Maude and Mack, lest they guess I'd been hunkered down at the door, listening.

"As for my thinness."

"You've been listening," they both said accusingly.

"Yes, I have. But that doesn't change what I'm saying. I think Louise is trying to destroy my life."

"You're just too imaginative," Mack said. "People don't do those things. Life isn't like that."

"You, a cop, can say that! You who know better than anybody the terrible things people do. You see it all the time."

"Hell hath no fury like a woman scorned," said Maude. "I can believe that Louise might do these things."

"He didn't scorn Louise," said Mack. "He went back to her. Ronda is the scorned one. She's the one who's been provoking Louise and I know that for a fact. All this other stuff is pure fancy."

"Mack, I can't *believe* what you're saying. Judas!"

"It's true, though. You know it's true, Ronda. Come back to reality. This isn't one of your stories. If you ask me, you've been behaving damned irrationally."

Mack was ranting at me now.

He seemed to have forgotten all about the sensitive artist angle.

He ranted on; it was a tirade. "What about Ishmael coming in your window? What's that all about, for God's sake? Why doesn't he come in the door?"

"I don't see what on earth that has to do . . ."

"Ishmael? Coming through your window?" Maude was looking at me in absolute amazement.

"I don't want to talk about it." I backed away, turned. "I'm going home."

"Who asked you down here anyhow?" Mack said. It was like a knife through my heart.

"Mack!" said Maude, sounding shocked.

"Well, she's been out there spying on us, hasn't she?"

I ran back up the drive to the lane and through the gate to my house, picking up the shopping bag en route.

I put away the marketing, muttering to myself. "Okay, let them all come and rape me and kill me. Who cares? Certainly my best friends don't care. They just want to talk about how weird I am. Here's Mack, a policeman, and he won't protect me, won't even make an ordinary inquiry, just takes the only clue and uses it to chop up his vegetables for God's sake. What does a crime matter when there's dinner to prepare? I hope when the Rapist comes he leaves his rope so Mack can use it for a clothesline. We victims have to keep the police force outfitted as best we can. Maybe he can use my blood to flavor his soup."

I realized I was chilled, my teeth were chattering. I was still in my damp running clothes. I stripped, showered, and enfolded myself in my Joseph's robe. I turned on the furnace. Then I combed my hair, put on some lip gloss. Now I only looked dismal around the eyes. I did want everything nice for Sam's last night.

It was my turn to make chopping sounds as I diced up the onions and mushrooms for the steak sauce.

"I'm sorry I shouted at you." Mack stood in the kitchen doorway.

I stood abashed. "Thank you. I apologize for spying on you."

"That's all right."

I attended to my chopping, awkwardly, having to be careful of my fingers.

"It's awful hot in here. I think you've got the furnace on."

"Because I'm freezing." I stopped chopping. "The reason I came down was—to see if you could have supper with me and Sam. It's his last night. But I guess you have plans . . . all that chopping . . ."

"Yeah, I do. But I'll come by in the morning to say good-bye to him. Oh, and Maude says she'd like you to come over to her house in the morning to talk. She has a dinner date now."

"Okay, that's cool."

Chopping sounds.

"We were just talking about you because we care about you, you know."

"I know. I won't come down another time unless I'm asked."

"I didn't mean that. You know I didn't mean what I said. I was just mad."

"If you care about me, you should believe me and protect me and not get mad at me," I said, trembly-voiced.

"What you need protection from is your own thoughts. I can't do anything about that except get mad about it. It's frustrating. You twist everything around. Now you think Louise poisoned Blue."

"I do think so. I wish I'd thought it before. I could have had an autopsy done. Now I can't because he was cremated. I'll never know. But that sudden paralysis. He had some arthritis all right, from his old war wounds, but there was no reason for his spine to just suddenly disintegrate like that. Poor Blue. And the coast was clear. I'm sure she knew Sam and I were off to the marathon. And you, too, were gone. Cut off in his prime he was, instead of being allowed to die in the ripeness of time."

"Fifteen is hardly a dog's prime."

"It was for Blue."

"Well, I gotta go. Have a nice dinner and tell Sam I'm sorry but I'll see him tomorrow. And look—one other thing,"

"Yes?"

"When you talk to Maude tomorrow, don't get swept away."

"Swept away?"

"You two get carried away. It's better for you to talk to me."

"But you don't believe me!"

"That's why it's better. I . . . I care about you as much as Maude does but I stay detached. Know what I mean? Dispassionate. I don't get drawn in."

"That's what I mean," I yelped. "You don't *believe* me!"

"That's what I mean too," he said.

3 . . .

A s it turned out, Ishmael called, so I invited him to dinner.

"God, it's hot in here."

"I have the ague. You can strip down to your T-shirt like Sam has, if you want."

It was a good dinner. Sam and Ishmael talked about running. They compared their times for the mile, the two miles, the five thousand meters. Their times were pretty similar. They decided to race each other in some footrace in August, when Sam got home from his summer job. Meanwhile Sam would give Ishmael a chance at the right-handed-home-dialing record.

After dinner Ishmael went at it with enthusiasm and we couldn't touch him. He was almost a full second faster at dialing—0:6:43. Sam and I couldn't even get out of the sevens and into the sixes. I left him and Sam to battle it out for the left-handed championship and washed up the dishes, musing the while.

Ishmael seemed more Sam's generation than mine.

Bachelors seemed so much younger than people even of the same age who have been married and had kids. It's as if life hasn't touched them deeply enough, I thought. They haven't had enough of blood and urine. It's not that they haven't suffered. It's that they haven't had enough of the mundane, the everyday dealing with other human beings; menstrual periods, dirty diapers, common colds, money worries. Mack wasn't so much older than Ishmael but he'd been to war and to marriage. It made a difference.

Ishmael had sunk into the mire, but that's not a place to gain in the understanding of life. You do not learn there. You literally get bogged down there. But, for sure, getting unbogged is a character-builder.

Bemused, I abandoned the dishes, wandered to my writing room, and made a poem.

> *Mire and War*
> *Some say you learn most in the mire*
> *Some say in bed.*
> *From what I know of marital romps*
> *I don't hold with those who favor swamps.*
> *I think I know enough of strife*
> *To say that war,*
> *For learning life,*
> *Has much to teach,*
> *On dung*
> *And gore,*
> *More dire than bed or mire is war.*
> *Much more.*

(With apologies to Robert Frost)
"That's good." Ishmael was reading over my shoulder. I hadn't heard him come into my room. Startled and embarrassed, I flipped the paper over. "What's the matter?" he asked.

"I hate people to read anything that's in progress." The poem was all crossed out, written over, under, and sideways. It was unreadable. "Especially a poem. It's got to be perfectly typed to be seen. To be heard."

"I didn't know you wrote poems."

"Well, I don't really. Just sometimes for fun. Verse really. Doggerel."

"Did you write that just now?"

"I wrote some in my head, doing the dishes, and it's still being written. I didn't hear you come in. Gee, you walk quietly."

"You were deep in concentration."

"Yes, I guess I was."

Sam walked in and said, "Thanks for the dinner, Mom. Real good. I'm going down to say good-bye to Mack, then I'm off to a party." He gave me a kiss.

"Okay, honey. Have fun. What time are you setting off for Klamath Falls?"

"Around eight."

"I'll roust you up."

"I guess I'll go along now, too," said Ishmael. "I should do some writing. I've got to get going on my songs. I don't know where the days go. I should just do it. Like you do. Just sit down and do it every day no matter what. Get concentrating deeply."

"That's right." I encouraged him to do so, gave him a pep talk.

"Okay, off I go. See you soon. Thanks for the dinner. I'm glad you've stopped shivering."

"It does me a world of good to write a poem. 'Bye, Ishmael."

I stayed at my writing table working over my poem. Time went by; I was very absorbed. Then fatigue hit me like a sledgehammer. And with it, fear.

Fatigue meant bed and bed meant, as Sam would say, pretty much—too scared to go to sleep.

I recollected that Ishmael had said, "I'll see you soon."

That could mean he planned to return tonight, knowing Sam was out.

I just wasn't up to hearing the window go up in any capacity. In fact I was just going to tell Ishmael to cut it out. I couldn't do that anymore. Either he would have to go with the biscuit-arousal scheme or go find some other woman's window. In fact, I would like to end the sexual element of our relationship, just be friends.

I would have to tell him why.

Why hadn't I discussed any of this rape business with Ishmael? I'd never once mentioned the Rapist to him, whereas I talked about it constantly with everyone else. I practically collared strangers on the street to talk about it. Why not with Ishmael? Because the idea must still be lingering on in my imagination that Ishmael and the Rapist were one. Tonight, when he had come upon me at my poem-writing, walking so noiselessly, it had flashed into my mind again. And I never had inquired of him how he learned my address, whether he had asked Maude for it. Time went by and it seemed such an out-of-context thing to ask. Now we'd been lovers for some weeks . . .

I shoved aside the typewriter so I could put my elbows on the table and slump there.

I thought of Maude's look of amazement when Mack told her about Ishmael and the window. It made me realize how very bizarre it was. If you do anything enough, it loses its strangeness. But then a look of amazement from a friend puts it back into perspective and you see that what you are having with Ishmael is not an ordinary romance.

Still, it's such a simple thing to let a man come in the window if he wants to. I was happy to oblige. Until now. Now the idea of that window going up even an inch gave me the willies.

Anything but that, I thought. He can come down the chimney if he wants. Or burst out of the refrigerator. The window. No. No more. It is locked for the duration.

A good resolution, if only that alone were enough to give me sleep. But it won't, I thought, because there will still be sounds at the window. I will forever hear sounds. And it might be Ishmael, or Louise pressing her broken nose against the glass, or the Rapist, or Moby come back at last. Whoever, whatever, I can't take it. What am I going to do? Sam goes tomorrow and I'll be alone again. It is intolerable to think that I've become one of those ladies afraid to sleep alone. Afraid to be alone. Trying to persuade friends to come for the night, or to let me go to their houses. Or worse, getting married just for the company.

What of my dream of being a feisty, independent person, invulnerable to old age, sickness, and loneliness? A lover of men, asking no quarter, a writer of stories, a runner of mountains, a grandmother of babies—what a wonderful picture of a possible future. Instead I am increasingly burdened by this stupid fear.

I sat at my writing table, head in hands.

Suddenly the turmoil of my thoughts was stilled. The roily waters of rape and fear drained from my brain and were replaced by the clear, calm pool of the simple and beautiful story regarding St. Francis and his beloved St. Blanche:

As a young girl, Blanche fled her family—and her impending marriage which had been arranged by them—for love of Francis. She cut off her hair and laid it at his feet, saying she wished to follow him. Francis knew he could not have a woman among his followers, especially one who loved him to such a frightening degree, and who caused such a frightening response in himself. So it was decided that she would go to a nunnery. Francis did not let himself see Blanche for twenty years, so great was his love and desire for her. But they kept in close touch, talking through intermediaries. Always he would ask her advice before taking any great decision. Finally the day came, shortly before his death, that he went to see her at the nunnery. Soon, a hue and cry was set up in the town, for a great light was seen over the church. "The nunnery is on fire!"

"No," said one of the monks. "It is only that Francis is inside, talking with Blanche."

What a beautiful story. I got up from my table, straightening it up, turned off the light, and went to the bedroom.

What a comfort it would be to believe in God and imagine that he was testing me, I thought as I disrobed, simply testing me by taking my loved ones from me one by one.

However, since I didn't and it wasn't, who was doing all these things to me? Louise?

4 . . .

*I*n the morning, as I stood in the lane saying goodbye to Sam, he said, "About the County Rapist, Mom."

"Yes?"

"Hang it up."

"I wish I could. I'll try to. But if anything *does* happen to me . . ."

"Nothing's going to happen," he scowled.

"Just listen to me a minute," I begged him. "I've made a will. You'll have the house and . . ."

"Come on, Mom!"

" . . . and enough money to see you through college."

Sam's friends were driving up the lane and I could see his relief. In a second he'd be saved from this hideous emotionalism.

" . . . and always remember how much I loved you," I said trying not to feel desperate that in two seconds he'd be gone, " . . . and . . . and . . . that I ran a marathon before you did. *Way* before."

He smiled and hugged me. "Okay. And I promise to tell your grandchildren all about it."

"Good-bye, sweetheart."

We kissed. " 'Bye, Mom."

I watched him drive away, then I hightailed it over to Maude's house for our talk. She would comfort me and clear up all my confusions. Everything would fall into place. I would stop trembling and see exactly how to proceed.

In a matter of minutes I was sitting at her kitchen table, sipping her good French-roast coffee and eating her hot apple pie. "Do you think it is Louise doing all these things to me?" I inquired of her. "She said I was a thorn. And mad as a hatter."

"She has good reason to think so since you threw that pot of geraniums at her in the town square."

"I keep forgetting about that. Curious how I do."

I reenvisioned the scene: how she had cut me and walked away, my ensuing surge of fury. Something about all that blood tidal-waving to my brain must have knocked out a couple of vital brain cells, the ones that otherwise allow me to remember my action, for it was almost as if I had amnesia about it. Whenever someone mentioned it, I stood astonished.

I remembered Louise's look of ineffable hatred after she looked over to me from the pot at her feet.

"I don't think you understand what a terrible thing that was for you to do to her, Miss. Primarily it was humiliating. And she's a proud woman. Such a thing as you did can have powerful repercussions."

I tried to put myself in Louise's place, to feel proud, first-ladyish, Mercedes-ful, designer-garbed, hair-styled, as I paraded through the town square on the arm of my distinguished husband, the mayor. I honored the town with my being, then suddenly sensed the airy rush of a weighty projectile, heard it crash at my heels. I turned, looked down to see a lowly geranium at my feet. Couldn't it at least be an orchid, I thought. (No, no, she wouldn't think that. She'd look down, not comprehending at first what had transpired here. Whence had this flower pot come? Then she'd look up and over to see Ronda Thompson standing in front of the flower shop, head held ridiculously high as if she were on the prow of a ship, as if she were a figurehead or modeling for one. That woman is mad as a hatter! she'd think. She's dangerous.)

Again I felt the flash of fear as I thought how easily it could have hit her, hurt her, killed her. She could have died from a bashed skull just as Alan did, and it would have been no less incredible. Only it wouldn't have been an act of nature, it would have been an act of murder.

From every pore the sweat burst from my body—as if I'd run all-out, or made love to Joe.

"What's the matter?" Maude was alarmed.

I put my head down. "Nothing. I feel faint."

Maude got me some water.

"It's just my imagination getting out of hand. Mack's right. He says I'm too imaginative. I was just carrying that scene forward in my mind. If I'd hit her with the pot . . ." I drank, shook myself free of visions. Powerful repercussions, Maude had said.

"You think I provoked her, then?" I asked Maude. "To come and get me in the middle of the night, with a knife? My gesture, after all, was impulsive. Hers was calculated, premeditated. I think if Sam hadn't been in that bed, I'd be dead now. And people would think it was the Rapist. When you think about what Joe said (when I first arrived, I'd told Maude about our interview on the mountain), "it's quite possible, probable even, that Louise means to kill me."

"Yes, it is," Maude said, considering, filling me with fear.

"What'll I do?" I quavered.

"I don't know. Now she is more angry and humiliated because of her broken nose and because you accused her of being the County Rapist. God, that poor woman: Mack isn't entirely off the beam when he says that you've been provoking the hell out of her. If you put yourself in her place . . ."

I was going to be damned if I'd put myself in her place for the fight in the bedroom. Being her, walking through the town square, was enough for one morning.

"Poor woman, my eye. You forget that she came through my window. With a knife!"

"What if she didn't?"

"Maude! What do you mean what if she didn't?"

"Okay, I believe you. I believe you. I just hope the hell she doesn't know you met Joe yesterday."

"I'm sure she doesn't. I was careful. There's no way she'll find out."

"If there's a way, she'll find it," Maude said direly. She looked at me anxiously. "Miss, I think you should try to talk to her."

"And say what?"

"Soothe her. Tell her you don't love Joe anymore. That it's all over. Tell her you love Ishmael. Do you love Ishmael?"

"Uh . . . I . . . No."

"What kind of relationship do you have with him? I thought it was platonic, that you just ran together and talked about his going to be a monk."

"We did. We still do. But now we're lovers too. Sort of. He's not really very loving and, worse, he doesn't let me be loving—meaning tender and affectionate. It's a weird relationship."

"He comes in the window and has sex with you and leaves."

"That's about the size of it." I hung my head.

"But, Ronda, that's awful! You can't let a man do that to you."

"It's not all his doing. I'm a party to it. I receive him gladly through the window into my arms. Although I must say it's getting me down a bit."

"It sounds very . . . unnatural. Not to say perverse."

"I haven't had much experience of men. How was I to know it wasn't the norm?"

"Are you serious?"

"No, it was just a little joke. By the way, this is a funny question, but did you ever tell Ishmael where I lived? I mean, did he ever ask you?"

"No, why?"

"Think back to when we got home from the marathon."

"No, I haven't seen him since then at all."

Maude laid another piece of pie on my dish and interrupted my thoughts. "If she came to kill you . . ." said Maude.

"Who?"

"Louise, of course. If she did come to try that, she failed and that was her only chance. She won't try again because she'd be the first suspect."

"But can we be sure she sees it that way? Maybe I should tell her that if she makes another attempt on my life . . . I mean if anything happens to me, you and Mack will know it's she. So she'd better not. She'd better back off. Would that be a good idea? I could write her a note. (Pleasing visions of throwing a note-encumbered rock through her window welled up in my mind once again.) Let's see . . ." I got out pen and paper from my bag and wrote: "Don't try anything more. Mack and Maude know all. Stay out of my life and house. Or else."

"It looks awfully like a threat to me," said Maude. "I don't think you want to be sending her threatening notes on top of everything else."

"On top of what else? What have I done?" (See! Once again I had forgotten the Geranium Incident.) "Nothing. I certainly am not going to be wishy-washy and intimidated by her." I considered. "Very well, how about this then?" I wrote, "The knife is in my hands now. Heh, heh." I didn't write down the heh heh, just made an expulsion of it to Maude, for effect. I didn't wait for her comment but went on writing. "Or this: 'The thorn has only begun to prick.' No, this: 'It takes a prick to feel a thorn.' Get it? She called me a thorn so I'm calling her a prick. It's not good, is it? Too labored. Well, something in a deeper vein. 'What is a broken nose compared to a broken heart?' "

"Ronda . . ."

I was scribbling wildly now all over the paper. " 'Everybody sees a broken nose. A broken heart is hidden from the world like the secrets of the womb.' Too heavy eh? Something catchy would be better. Something to stick in her mind. Oh boy, look at this one: 'A broken head and you'd be dead. It was a broken pot instead.' Now that's really good. That's terrific, I think. Don't you?"

Maude took the paper and crumpled it up.

"I was only kidding," I said. "More of my little jokes. Heh, heh."

Spasmodically I grabbed another piece of paper from my bag. "I'll be serious now. 'Dear Louise,'" I wrote. " 'Please understand for your own good, that Sergeant Scher is my neighbor and will be keeping an extremely close watch on my house and person. Despite his rather exaggerated politeness to you the other evening, he is fully aware of your animosity toward me and his concern for my safety is massive. He is a close friend and, as well, has a unique understanding of the sensitivity of the artist. An artist needs a safe and salubrious place in which to create . . .'"

"Wait!" I cried. "This is getting too elaborate. It won't fit on a rock."

"A rock?" Maude asked, bewildered. "Fit on a rock?"

"I didn't mean to say that. I don't know why I said that or even thought it. I take it back about the rock. Oh dear." I crumpled the paper up. "I just don't know what to do."

"Well, if anyone's going to throw a rock at her, let it be me. You had your chance with the geraniums. Now it's my turn. Nothing's going to stop her," Maude went on, looking suddenly fierce. "If she's consumed by jealousy, she'll do anything to hurt you."

"Like getting Blue and Moby."

"Yes! And she will feel justified because she convinces herself that it is all in the name of love. She feels Joe *belongs* to her. You can only be jealous if you are possessive enough to see a person as property. So you have the fact that she imagines her hateful, hostile feelings to be love. She believes she owns Joe. She believes that you have harmed her in innumerable ways, harmed and worse—humiliated her. Therefore she feels she has every justification in the world to torment you and, I suppose, actually to kill you. That's why she could hold her head up so successfully the other night—because she felt herself to be completely in the right. She doesn't consider you as a feeling human person at all."

I sat immobilized by this sudden vehement flow of words from Maude, my eyes and jaws agape. This was comfort?

Finished, she rose decisively from the table. "I'm afraid I have to go to work now. Why don't you try to get Ishmael to spend the nights with you? That way you'll at least have a man around to protect you. Has he ever spent the night?"

"Once. Do you have any Bisquick?"

"No, I make my biscuits from scratch."

"Okay. I'll buy some Bisquick and try to get Ishmael to spend the night."

Maude rolled her eyes and shook her head. "When do you make him the biscuits? Before or after?"

"Before. Doesn't everyone?"

In this way I eked out a last little joke, trying to keep suspended the slim spiderweb of spirit left in me.

Walking home, I saw Louise behind every bush.

But at least I didn't see Joey and Ishmael rounding every corner.

5 . . .

When I got home, I called the Mastersons' house. Joe answered so it must have been Saturday.

"I'd like to speak to Louise," I told him, not even saying hello.

"Why don't you just give me the message, Ronda?"

"I want to speak to Louise."

After a few minutes Louise came on the line. "Yes?"

"This is Ronda Thompson. Just tell me one thing, Louise. Did you kill my dog?"

In reply to my question came a singular noise. It was like the cry of an enraged and wounded dinosaur, or as I would imagine such a cry to have sounded in some saurian yesteryear. I could hear the cries—more human-sounding now—continuing on into the distance. Then Joe's voice returned to the line. "What did you say to her?"

"I asked her if she killed Blue. I'm most certain now that Blue was poisoned. I rue the day I condoned cremation. If I'd buried him in my yard I could dig the old boy up and . . ."

"Ronda," said Joe gently. "I realize that I have hurt you very badly and I won't ever forgive myself . . ."

"No. No, that's not true!"

"Just let me finish. I know this has been a hard time for you. Naturally I have made allowances . . ."

"Allowances! Just a minute here . . ."

His voice hardened. "But now you have gone too far. I was wrong to have met you yesterday and to have said the things I said. It is better to sever all . . ."

"That woman is after my life!" I butted in. "She doesn't just want part of it, the part that is you; she wants all of it: my Blue, my Moby, and my blood. Last of all my life's blood. You understand why that would be *last*."

I could still hear thin wailing sounds in the background. It must be hard for her to wail and also try to hear Joe's end of the conversation (which I knew she wouldn't miss for the world), but that was one capable woman.

"It's amazing to me," I said, "that my simple question could spark off hysteria just now when she was calm as a cucumber for a whole hour the other night. With you she plays the poor, frail, beleaguered woman in need of a protector. With me and Mack she played the Lord High Executioner. Maybe she's a Jekyll-and-Hyde personality. Maybe she *is* the Rapist. Better that than a dog murderer and blood-letter. Maybe . . ."

"I'm going to hang up now, Ronda. You asked me to stop loving you and try instead to recreate my marriage. That's what I am going to do."

"I asked you that?"

"Yes."

"But you wouldn't hang up on me, Joe?"

"I'm sorry." The phone clicked. He did hang up on me. Joe. He hung up. On me. My Joe.

For the first time I canceled Gramps' Night. I wasn't up to making conversation. Or soup. I decided that a good hard run would be the best thing that I could do now—the only thing. I put on my Nike Elites, my blue Dolphin shorts, my yellow marathon T-shirt. I would run the Dipsea trail to Stinson Beach; the Dipsea, which every runner knows is the hardest trail to run in the whole world. Although it is only 7.1 miles, it goes from sea level to sea level and there is a mountain in between.

It starts with 671 steps that are etched into the side of the first ridge. At the top of them is Windy Gap, so called because a hurricane blast of wind tries to knock you off your legs that have become like jelly anyhow from the staired ascent. The route reads like *Pilgrim's Progress*: Dynamite Hill, Cardiac Hill, Insult Hill, Slough of Despond. All the hills are straight up, and uniquely, they don't have a down side to them. But it is Hog's Back Rise, the least steep, that takes the heart out of you because it is so long and pitiless. It is unyielding, implacable, and cruel. It is a treadmill, it never ends, Samson at the mill wheel, and who wants it to end, when there's Cardiac to get up when it does? Before Cardiac is the Rain Forest, so named because it is always dark and dripping, no matter how sunny the day. And it is thundering too. There is always thunder in the rain forest, which is the sound of your own blood pounding in your ears.

But oh! Oh boy! If you can get up Cardiac and you have any energy left at all, then, oh then will come the run of your life. It is called Swoop Hollow and Steep Ravine but it should be called Exhilaration Hill and Ecstasy Arroyo. There is the vast blue Pacific spread out before you to the very ends of the earth. There on the open hills are a superabundance of flamboyant orange poppies that knock your eyes out, as well as purple lupin and, for fauna, golden deer and black Angus there on the high grassy hills above the sea.

And you run, how you run, down to the glittering sea, a seeming sub-four-minute-mile pace. And oh yes, there is still Insult Hill to get over, but that is no more than a bump in the road by now, you scorn it, you humiliate it. And steps? Yes, there are more steps, hundreds, but you take them four at a time and then over some stiles, fences, creeks, dirt, and asphalt and you are there on the sea-scented sand.

Runner's high? You didn't know the meaning of the words until now, when you have run, have subdued, the terrible Dipsea in an hour and seven minutes, your best time. Others at the beach, on grass, coke, or brine, are nowhere near as spacey as you who are on air and heroics.

I sat on the sand and watched the waves wash in, pull back, roll reliably on. I let all the imponderabilia of life wash through my mind with a similar ebb and flow. My mind, elated from the run, empty of calculation, was open to the soothing influence of wave action, fascinating and monotonous, the two main ingredients for hypnosis. I sat bewitched, charmed, at peace. For a long time I sat gaga by the sea.

It seemed to do me good. It seemed to do me lots of good. My little spiderweb of spirit maybe got a strengthening strand before its disintegration into utter cobwebhood. I should have stayed longer by the sea, a day, a week, just to repair myself a bit. I should have checked into the Sandpiper Motel and stayed.

Oh, if only I could have stayed there by the healing sea, the nourishing mother of us all. But I didn't. I hitchhiked home.

6 . . .

*B*ack at my house, I found a big manila packet that someone had left in my mailbox. I took it in and set it on my work table until I could shower and change into something warm. With the coming of evening it had turned cool and I didn't want to get the ague again. I stood a long while under the bursting waters, then put on my purple pants and black turtleneck sweater. I poured a cup of coffee from what was left in the morning pot and opened the packet. It was pictures. Eight-by-ten blowups. There was a note attached which said simply, "Telephoto lens. Joey."

My heart sank into my socks. I felt such dismay. He'd gotten me. Taken me. Captured me.

I was Joey's now. Joey's creature. And there was nothing in the world I could do about it. I was powerless. Joey was an inexorable force: Even a woman who could run the Dipsea in an hour and seven could not contend with his determination to invade my life. Invade. Yes. To invade is to enter forcefully and take possession. Maybe Joey was the rapist I had feared.

I felt so paralyzed with dismay that I did not even look at the pictures. How, I wondered, could I have had the physical courage to run that Dipsea so hard only hours ago and now feel so broken, so uncouraged.

After a while—I don't know how much of a while but my coffee was long cold—I roused myself enough to look listlessly at the pictures. There were twenty-five of them, all taken during my "week of grace." It was like looking at pictures of another woman, or of myself as a young woman, so far away from that week did I feel now.

However, the photographs were breathtaking.

They were dated, each one, but I would have recognized that week by my happiness. My glow. Yes, there was a nimbus of light over my head in each picture in varying degrees. In some you'd hardly see it if you weren't looking for it, especially in the forest pictures where the light was so remarkable anyhow, streaming down through the branches of redwoods. Dazzling! And in some the halo got lost in the sky.

There were many taken of me running on the mountain with Ishmael—in the woods and over the grassy knolls. Then there were pictures of me going about the more mundane aspects of my life: coming out of the town market with a bag of groceries, out of the library with books, at the track with the old-timers, and at soup—he must have come a second Gramps' Night. In the last photos Joey got closer to home, but not inside. I am taking the mail from my box, clipping a rose from the bush by my door, sinking my nose deep into it. Lastly there was a picture of the house at night, taken from above. Joey must have been up a tree or a phone pole. Now it is the house that glows. What a dear little house. A storybook house. You can even see a hint of smoke issuing from the chimney and light from almost every window. Hold! What is that by my bedroom window? It's a figure!

A figure is standing in the dark by my bedroom window!

All the fine hairs along my spinal column were winging it. This was the scariest picture I had ever seen. The sweet glowing hominess of the house, seeming to enfold the lurking villainous figure by its window, was a matrix that chilled me to my marrow.

But wait! My horror turned to excitement. The date upon the picture was the night Louise had come. Proof! Now I would have proof that indeed the venomous woman had entered through the window with intent to rape or kill. Ishmael had not come here that night, so there would be no confusion. We would blow up the picture some more. We would blow up the picture within an inch of its life until it divulged its shadowy secret, until the figure proved itself unquestionably to be Louise. Then let's hear her lie her way out of that one. Ho ho! Then we'll let her manifest her mayoressness and Mercedesness until the cows come home and see where it gets her.

I packed up the picture and ran with it down to Mack's house.

7 ...

*H*e was home. "Proof!" I cried. "Mack, we're in business. By a most marvelous fluke a ... er ... person took a picture of my house the night Louise came and it shows a figure by my bedroom window. All we need to do, Mack, old boy, is blow the picture up some more and we'll have Louise in all her glory."

"Hmmnnn, let me see that. There's a figure there all right. A human figure for sure. Hmmn. Pretty amazing."

"Pictures don't lie, Mack. You can't say I'm imagining this now, can you? Even my powerful imagination can't impale a figure on film inside another person's camera."

Mack stroked his missing beard and studied the picture and hummed and hawed and presently said, "I'll get this to the lab first thing tomorrow. We'll blow it up and see what we've got. Meanwhile, are you keeping your house locked up tight?"

"Yes I am. Because the fact is, Mack, I'm feeling awfully scared."

"Is it locked now?"

"No, I just ran down . . ."

"Keep it locked at all times when you're in or out of it. Windows too."

"I will. I'll go and lock it now. You'll let me know, won't you, as soon as you have the blowup?"

"You bet."

"Oh, thank God. What a relief it will be to know. It will give me strength. Knowledge is such a . . . a buttress."

"If you get too scared," he said as I went out the door, "just come down to my place, okay? You know where the key is. You'll be plenty safe here."

"All right. That sounds like a good idea. Maybe I'll do that. Thanks, Mack. Thanks."

Back in the house, doors and windows locked, I made myself a cheese omelette and some french dressing to pour into the seed hole of an avocado half. I took my meal into the living room but couldn't muster the energy to produce a fire. I sat in front of the cold hearth and nibbled the food. I didn't feel very well.

Cobwebhood.

Some little time later there was a loud knocking at the door.

Startled, I scrambled up. I flicked on the outside light, for in the meantime night had come, and I went to the door and peered through the windowpanes of it. Joey Horgan stood there. Wordlessly we eyeballed each other through the glass. He wore jeans, a heavy sweater, and a jaunty hat. His hands hung by his side, cameraless. I opened the door.

He sauntered in, chest out, shoulders swinging, eye-balls swiveling. "Hiya!" he said.

"Hello, Joey."

"Well, what didya think of them?"

"I think they are absolutely beautiful."

"I told ya. Didn't I tell you how good I am? Those pictures are not only absolutely beautiful, they are fantas-tically unusual and, what's more, with those pictures, with this Phot-o-graphic Essay (he drew it out, relishing the words) I, Joey Horgan, am going to become unbelievably famous.

"However, I still gotta get the house, the interiors, to complete the essay, wind it up, you know what I mean?" He fixed me with an angry eye. (The other eye just kept looking around the house.) "You been locking the doors and win-dows," he accused me. "Not that there'd be much point in me takin' the pictures without you in them, but I like to come and get a feel of the place—so I can compose the pictures in my mind beforehand. Yeah."

By saying yeah, he agreed with himself. Joey listened carefully to everything he said.

"Joey, I love these pictures. I respect your art. But I'm not going to let you take pictures of me in the house and I'm not going to let you publish these. I'm sorry but . . ."

"Sorry?" Joey laughed a deep, pleased chuckle. "What're you sayin', girl? Come on, you don't tell me what I do and don't do. You don't have no say. None at all."

"Of course I do. It's my life. You have no right to take it and use it for your own ends."

"You bet your ass I can. You can't refuse me my art. I don't need your fuckin' permission. Tell me something—do you ask permission of everyone you write about? Do you consider their feelings?"

"I don't write *about* people. I create my characters—maybe from people I know but, if so, their real selves are sifted through my imagination and they become invented characters."

"That's good. A good explanation. And I have invented you. I created you in these pictures, right? You are my subject. My object. No, subject is a better word because it means you are two things to me: the subject matter of my picture and my subject in that I have dominion over you. Haha! I like it. You are under my rule, girl. Yeah, that's good. Real good!"

He stopped looking at me and roamed around the room, "getting the feel," I presumed.

"Well pin a rose on you. Don't break your arm patting yourself on the back, you goddamn egomaniac."

Those were not the fighting words they look like on paper because they came out on a quavery cobwebby voice. I had no fight left in me.

"Relax," he said. "I don't see why you can't relax and enjoy it."

"I can't because you have created this saintly Ronda who is not me. You've altered me and people will believe it."

"They can believe it or not believe it. What do I care?"

"You don't. But I care enormously."

"You're nothing to me. But these pictures are everything. They're great. Give in. You know I'm going to finish the essay. You know I'm going to get the pictures somehow. All you have to do is go about your business. You won't even notice me here. I become invisible when I work. And quiet as a mouse."

"I don't care if you act like a bulldozer. That's not the point. The point is the end product, this absurd lie that you'll be casting out into the world . . ."

"Hey! Hey! Just a minute now." He grabbed hold of me. He took my chin in one hand, hard, and brought his face right up next to mine, staring into my eyes. "One thing you gotta know, because everyone knows it and you do too. Here's what it is. Pictures don't lie. Right?"

8 . . .

No sooner was Joey out the door than the phone rang and it was Ishmael. "Can I come over?" he asked.

Good, I thought. Ishmael will not let Joey back in. He is bigger and stronger than Joey by far. And I'll be safe from Louise as well. He will protect me tonight from all comers. But there was one problem. "Yes," I said, "I'd love to have you come over but you'll have to come to the door."

"Why?"

"The window is locked. So is the door for that matter. But I'll let you in."

"But I want to come in the window. I'm hot."

"I'm sorry, you can't. I'll explain why when you get here. But I'm not unlocking the window even for a second and I'm just not up to your coming through it. It has nothing to do with you." (Or does it, I wondered.)

"What's the point of my coming if I can't come in the window? I don't want to come then."

"Ishmael, please come. I need you. I need your help."

There was a silence.

"Ishmael, I've never asked anything of you before."

My heart sank. I realized he would not respond to my plea, that in fact it was having the opposite effect. He was like a little boy not getting his way. It enraged me. But I needed him. I decided to lure him, hating myself for having to devise such a lowly strategem, hating *him* because I knew it would work.

"I have some fantastic pictures of you I want you to see."

"Do you? Who took them?"

"A professional photographer. They're of us running."

"I've always wanted a good picture of me running. Are they really good?"

"Unbelievable."

"I'd like to see them. Okay. I'll come on by."

"That's great, Ishmael. See you soon. Hurry over. Hurry!"

I paced nervously. Once Ishmael got here I knew I could relax. He was bigger than Joey; bigger even than Louise. Neither of them would dare to force entry with Ishmael here. But would he stay? I'd better get the biscuit batter mixed up so he'll see it. And get out the honey. He hates it to be cold from the refrigerator.

I mixed up two cups of Bisquick with the two-thirds cup of milk. What else? Oh yes, it wouldn't hurt to look nice. I took off my pants and sweater and put on a dress. I brushed my hair, shadowed my lids, glossed my lips.

Looking good, I felt a little better.

When Ishmael arrived, he had no eyes for me. "Where are the pictures?" he asked right away.

I got them out—the ones of the two of us.

He was enchanted with them. He went off into a poetic flight about their beauty, their art, their truth. He could not stop looking at them. He pored minutely over each one, monologuing away, free-associating as to what each picture meant for him. The only thing that seemed to mar the pictures at all for him was that I, too, was in them. But he seemed pretty able to block me out of his mind's eye. In fact, Mr. Religion didn't even notice the halo which, had he seen it, must have intrigued him a little, though probably, had he seen it, he would have figured it was *his* halo which the wind from the speed of our passage had blown over to my head.

"Look at this one. Put wings on my feet and I could be Mercury. I really should have done something with my looks. I still should. I don't mean be an actor or a model, but do something good with them. Preach the word of God. A lot of people would listen to me because of how I look, people who otherwise wouldn't care. Jesus must have been beautiful-looking, don't you think? Huh, Ronda? For people to have followed him so readily? It's not too late. I'm just thirty. Jesus was thirty-two when he . . ."

"Died," said I. "That's probably why he gave himself up to Pilate. He felt his looks were going. So his days as a preacher were numbered anyhow."

"What's the matter with you?"

He was holding one of the pictures up and actually covering me with his hand so as to see himself better.

"Why don't you just crop me out, Ishmael? Here, wait a minute, I'll get some scissors."

"Crop you out? What are you talking about?"

"Just cut me out of the pictures so they'll be unblemished. Only the magnificence of you will remain. Of course it will be hard to cut me out of those ones where we're running stride for stride but . . ."

"Ronda, you're behaving kind of funny, aren't you?"

"No, I'm serious. Crop me out of your whole life while you're at it."

He put the pile of pictures on the table and gave me his attention. "That's why you got me over here, isn't it? To dump me. You don't want to see me anymore. You're tired of me."

"No. I hoped that you might stay here with me tonight, as a friend. I need your help."

He grew excited. "You want to get rid of me, don't you? I don't mean anything to you."

"Of course you mean something to me. I'm very fond of you. But I don't want you to come through the window anymore. I want it to be different with us. I want to be friends, the way we originally were. It was better then."

"It's good now. We have nice times together. Because you're good to me. No woman's ever been so nice." He grew stubborn, crossed his arms, planted his feet. "I won't go."

I laughed. "I'm not asking you to go. I want you to stay." I kept laughing. I couldn't stop.

Ishmael looked more and more hurt with me. I went to the sink and splashed cold water on my face. I was really tempted to splash it on his face too.

"Can't you just say what you mean?" He'd followed me to the kitchen sink.

"I'm trying to." I was still giggling.

"Who was that man that was here a little while ago?"

I stopped laughing abruptly. The funniness shriveled up inside me. "Man? Here? How do you know there was a man here earlier?" I remembered the day I'd seen him rounding the corner. "Do you spy on me sometimes?"

"I come by when I want to. It's a free country."

"That first night you came by. How did you know where I lived? Had you followed me home one time?"

"Yeah, that's right. From the track."

"*Before* we met in Paradise Produce?" I was amazed. Then he amazed me more.

"I followed you there too. But the first time was when I saw you at the track with the old people. I was interested. What's the matter with that? Why all these questions? I have a right to come by when I want to."

"You have no right in the world to spy on me. I can't stand the thought of it." I was starting to recommence trembling. "Let me try to explain this one thing. I'm very nervous these days. And nothing makes me more nervous than the idea of you or of anyone prowling around my house unbeknownst to me. And the idea of your coming through the window absolutely terrifies me—even if I know for sure it's you."

"Who else would it be? That guy? I've seen him more than once around here."

Did Ishmael do nothing but watch this house?

I wondered if Ishmael had seen Louise prowling around as well as Joey. I had this vision of the three of them continually circling my house like vultures, spying on me and on each other.

"The reason I wanted you to come over . . ." I said softly and sensibly, hugging myself to try to still the stupid trembling. "The reason I want you here now, this evening, is to keep that very man from coming in. I don't want him ever to come in this house again."

"So there was something between you."

"No, nothing sexual or romantic." I was afraid to tell Ishmael that "the man" was the photographer, for fear he'd want to meet him, would welcome him into my house with open arms and urge him to take more pictures, this time just of him.

I was beginning to feel cobwebby again. If only Ishmael would just shut up and hug me and tell me he was my friend and protector and that the last thing he wanted in the world was for me to be scared and trembling and unhappy. That's what Joe would have done. But Joe had hung up on me.

"Ishmael . . .?" I prepared to plead. But he was wanting and needing encouragement too—his kind.

"Then prove to me that you like me," he said. "Let me come to you through the window. Prove it to me now. Be there for me like you have been, with your arms open to me. I want you all soft and moist and open to me. And moaning. Please! It works so well."

"No. No, I can't. I can't do that anymore. No. I'm sorry. I just want to be friends now."

Ishmael grabbed me tensely. "Don't say that."

"Let go of me, Ishmael."

"Don't say that then. You can't just drop a person. You can't turn cold to a person and treat them like dirt. Look at me!"

"I am looking at you."

"You're not. Your eyes are but there's nothing behind them."

"Ishmael, you're hurting me." I wrenched out of his grasp. Talk about eyes. His weren't connecting at all. It was like that time on the mountain. He looked disturbed—with that same strange combination of distress and glee. I was frightened. I tried to speak gently. "I'm not dropping you. I . . ." As I spoke, I backed away, putting the studio couch between us. He lunged over it, grasped me by the shoulders. We both fell onto the floor. "Hey!" I cried. "Easy! What are you doing? Ouch!" I tried to scramble up but he held me, pulled me down beneath him. "Ishmael, stop! No!" He covered my mouth with his hand, his forearm on my breast, holding me down. With the other hand, he wrenched off my panties, unloosed his jeans. I struggled. I wriggled and twisted and kicked. I was helpless.

"Be nice to me, Ronda," he said. "You've always been so good. I don't like you this way. What are you doing? Can't we just fuck? Oh God, can't we just fuck?"

I was helpless. His muscles that I had so admired were turned against me. His penis that I'd caressed like a pet had become a weapon. It felt like a rod, a burning rod thrust up into me, so hard and so long, it reached all the way up through my entrails into my heart, cleaving me. My entire body felt cleft in two by that hard, hot, inhuman shaft.

I thought of the burning rod laid on St. Francis's eyes, of his gentleness and courage. I stopped struggling. I pray you be courteous with me, I murmured over and over again in my mind. A litany. I thought of ocean waves. I tried to hypnotize myself out of what was happening to me. I pray you . . .

Ishmael continued shouting while he humped me. "What's the matter with you? Why are you being like this? Why can't you be nice?"

It was endless. He would never finish. I thought of oil wells going up and down, into the ground, deeper and deeper, in and out. What was Ishmael digging for, driving for? What did he hope to find? He'd already reached the end of me. Couldn't he feel that he'd reached the end?

"Be nice, Ronda. Be nice to me."

He gushed. "Aheeiah?" he cried, as if he'd run his own sword through himself.

I pray you . . .

He did not collapse on me. He froze and withdrew right away. He stood up, zipped his fly, buckled his belt. He said, "You'll be sorry. You'll be sorry you did this to me, Ronda."

I heard the door close. I lay there, afraid to move, afraid that if I did move my body would fall apart in the two pieces it had been carved in. I thought that if only I could lay there a little while, my body might grow together again into one piece. My head was in one piece, I was pretty sure of that. It was like the marathon, only my head left to keep me going.

Why don't you call Mack? a voice in my head asked me.

I can't, I answered. I can't. And then I wept.

I lay there on my back, still not moving, my skirt tangled around my waist, and I cried. Cried, not for having been raped, but for not being able to tell Mack. Or that's how it seemed to me. Maybe I cried for Joe, too, for the loss of love, for Blue and Moby. I cried for my frailty—for all the hard running in the world that wasn't going to make me as strong as a man. Finally I cried so hard that the sobs racked my body into movement and I did not fall into two pieces. I saw that I was still whole. And that was a great relief to me. It brought immeasurable relief.

I got to my feet then and ran a hot bath. I lay in the tub for a long time until the skin of my fingers began to wrinkle. Then I put on my robe and sat on the edge of my bed in a stupor.

Sorry? Ishmael assures me I'll be sorry, seeming to point to some future state of sorriness, although how I could be any sorrier than I am right now I can't imagine. I'm mostly sorry I ever met Ishmael, ever spoke to him that day in Paradise Produce. I shall now become not only the town peculiar and lone juice drinker but the person who never, on any account, for any amount of money, no matter how pressing the need, will speak to a stranger. How right I was to have turned instinctively away from him, turned to the tangerines. Why didn't I remain with my head down until he went away? And then, to think that later I went looking for him. That certainly was a sorry move. I certainly am sorry about that one.

You'd think I'd feel the worst had already occurred. that I couldn't feel any sorrier, that Ishmael's threat could hold no terror for me now. But it did. I sat on the bed, perfectly still as if waiting for something more. I still felt threatened. I felt, deep in my heart, that this night would be the end of me, that there was more to come, and that waiting for whatever was going to happen was intolerable. There was still the knife-wielding Louise; Joey, who was so relentless; the County Rapist, black and silent. All around me were lies and violence, people insisting themselves into my life and body. And I had nothing left to fight with—my body in a stupor, my mind stupid, a stupid creature in sorry shape. I should try to get up, move around, bestir myself.

I did. I rose to my feet and walked around unsteadily like an accident victim who, after months of physical therapy, takes her first steps without crutches.

Leaving the house lights ablaze, I tottered out my front door, through the gate, across the street, and down to Mack's place . . . for sanctuary.

And Threatened With Jail

1 ...

Mack's place was dark. Getting the key from beneath the stone of the bonsai, I let myself in. Without Mack there, his place seemed cellarish: small, chilly, poorly lit.

I sat awhile in abject misery.

In his closet, smartly hung, was a uniform fresh from the cleaners. My heart lifted as I conceived the plan of putting it on and going back to my house, wearing it. I would much rather be in my warm and cheery house than here in this dark bin. If I was disguised as Mack, I would feel that I was secure from intruders. Nothing would frighten away a person with evil intentions faster than the merest glimpse of a police uniform.

The idea worked miracles. I began to feel much better. Fear rolled away from me like water off duck feathers. I actually smiled as I got into Mack's uniform. I felt like a kid playing dress-up. Mack, at five feet eight, was not a tall man and, being a runner, he was slim. The uniform would not be terribly big for me. I remembered how Mack was worried about getting into the police academy because of his shortness. But they'd recently made a rule to allow for Orientals and it allowed for Mack too.

Still, the uniform swam on my hundred-and-five-pound frame. I rolled up the cuffs of the shirt and pants, pulled the belt in snug. By piling my hair up, the hat fit me pretty well.

When I get home, I thought pleasurably, I can fashion a badge out of foil.

I wondered whether to take his off-duty gun too. It would certainly give me an air of authority although, without the holster, it would not give an air of verisimilitude.

But who would check for details? No one. It was the all-over impression I wished to achieve. As long as I could give an immediate and vital impression of The Law, all would be well.

I tucked the gun in my belt.

I felt transformed. Not that I felt like Mack. No. Better. I felt like Ronda as she once was. The Ronda of yore. Ronda in all her intelligence, strength, and fearlessness. Not the craven creature jumping at her own shadow who'd slunk down to Mack's a half-hour ago to lick her sores.

I stood tall, head up. I swaggered around Mack's tiny quarters and then, still swaggering, went out the door, across the lane, through my gate, and up the brick walk to my door.

I went inside and took five minutes to make a badge of cardboard and aluminum foil which I pinned onto my shirt pocket. I admired myself for several minutes in the long mirror before realizing that the blue and yellow Nike elites didn't do. I got out an old pair of black espadrilles, rope-sole shoes, which did a little better.

Feeling really good now, I decided to go out and patrol around my house in case anybody was lurking. I did a good imitation of Mack's unremarkable walk several times around the house, then posted myself at the door.

Time began to slow down again as my rush of excitement and pleasure diminished. I began to wish something would happen. I began to feel like an ass, standing there on my stoop in Mack's uniform. What was the point of it all, really? What about sleep? And what about the next night?

What about my whole life? How was I to put in four hours of
writing each morning if I was to be up all night being Mack?
Really this was too stupid! I wasn't being the intelligent
Ronda of yore at all. The intelligent Ronda would not solve
a dilemma by playing dress-up. She would confront her
difficulty head on.

I'm not sure how or when or why I formed my next
decision, but the upshot of it was that I found myself in my
Honda with the engine going.

As I drove out the lane a police car was driving in.
Probably dear old Mack was cruising by my house to be sure
all was well. Good thing I wasn't still standing on the stoop.

2 . . .

*T*he next thing I knew I was behind, and partly
underneath, a bush at Joe's house with a rock in
my hand, trying to compose a note for it and having a strong
sense of *déjà vu*, as if I'd been through this whole scene
before. Twice I'd seen Joe pass in front of the lighted
windows of the monolithic house.

Okay. Here's what would happen. I would think of a
pungent message, secure it to the rock, throw the rock
through the window, being careful not to hit either of them.

Louise would call the police. She would be absolutely
astounded at how fast the police arrived since the police
would be me. "You called?" I would say, having rung the
doorbell the minute she put down the phone.

I began to giggle. It was delicious. What a joke. At first
she'd think it was a real policeman, if undersized. Then
she'd think it was Virginia Woolf in drag. It would be a few
seconds before she'd be blinded by the truth—that it was
her nemesis.

As I was thinking this and chuckling to myself, I began to hear the thin, high, unmistakable wail of distant sirens. I stopped laughing and listened. The sound was growing louder. How could this be?

How could the police have been called before I even threw the rock?

It was amazing. Like that other time when I didn't throw the rock and Louise told Mack later that I had. The woman, like me, obviously had precognitive powers. She could see into the goddamn future.

Well, all right. I was never one to be bound to the present. Not me. I could leap ahead into the immediate future with her if that was what she wanted. I was up for that.

I would give up the rock-throwing entirely and go directly into the next sequence. I would astound her by arriving at her door before the sirens even arrived in her driveway.

I scrambled out from under the bush, busted loose up the walk to the big mahogany door of the great stone house. Where is the moat, I wondered. How come no moat?

I rang the bell which gonged but I could hardly hear it against the noise of the arriving police cars.

The door began to open. Too late I realized I still held the rock—a small boulder, actually. Talk about lack of verisimilitude. I could get away with the espadrilles, the foil badge, and the off-duty gun tucked in the belt. But the rock? Nevertheless, I would carry it off as well as I could. Car doors were slamming behind me and footsteps were on the moat, I mean the path, as Joe opened the door to me.

Time stood still. It was high time that it did. I could see Joe trying to comprehend the figure at his door. I looked for Louise. I had wanted her to be the one to answer, not Joe. At the same time (the same still-standing time) I saw comprehension dawn in Joe's eyes and with it his face registered wild alarm. Our eyes seemed to lock together in an instant of excruciating agony. I broke off the look, trying to see beyond him to Louise. She must be somewhere. He seemed to be purposely blocking the door. Oh well, I would proceed with the program.

I fixed him with a dreadful, lawful eye and said, "You called?"

3 . . .

I was seized. Hands grabbed me from behind. My rock fell to the stoop. I was cuffed. Cuffed! Apprehended I was. Joe stood there. He couldn't hang up on this one. No way to terminate this scene with a click. What would he say? Do? Nothing. He stood there.

"Sorry about this, Joe. I'll take care of it."

Mack.

He wheeled me around, trotted me hastily down the walk. I twisted around to look back at Joe. He wasn't watching. He'd gone back into the house, closed the door.

Mack thrust me into the car. It was just him and just one police car. I had imagined a whole fleet deploying themselves around Joe's house and the neighborhood swarming with the force. But no. Just Mack. We cruised down the hill silently. No siren now.

I slumped wearily in the seat next to Mack. At least he hadn't put me behind the grill. He reached over and unlocked the handcuffs, passed me a handkerchief. I guess I was crying.

He drew up in front of the city hall, which incorporated the fire station and the police station.

"Do you want to go to jail?"

"Yes." There didn't seem any reason for me to carry on in society. I couldn't think of one reason. "I want to be executed too."

"I'm going to give you a choice," Mack said, not looking at me so he could sound severe—dear, dear person. "I can book you for misrepresenting oneself as a police officer, which is a misdemeanor carrying a $2500 fine or six months in jail . . ."

"Or both," we said in unison.

"Or I can choose to forget about it and take you home. I'll do that on one condition. That you obey my orders. That you let me take charge of you and your life for as long as I want. That you'll go to work for me."

"Work for you? Doing what?"

"Catching the Rapist."

"Are you serious?"

"Yes. I have an idea. But I won't spell it out for you now. You're too out of it."

"Would I get to keep wearing the uniform?" I asked hopefully.

"No." Mack sighed.

"I really feel good in this uniform. Safe."

"Well, which is it going to be, Ronda?"

"You'd really throw me in jail?"

"Yes I would."

"I'll do anything you say."

"Good." He started the engine. "I'll explain about it in the morning. Right now you're going to bed and I'm sleeping on your couch."

"How'd you know I was up at Joe's?" I asked as we motored through the midnight town. "Did Joe call the police?"

"No. I saw you driving away from the lane. I saw both our doors open. I saw my uniform gone when I checked my place. It wasn't exactly a three-pipe problem. I'm beginning to know how your mind works."

"But why the siren?"

"I was in a hurry. Like I said, I'm beginning to know how your mind works."

You Become

1 ...

I slept for fourteen hours. When I awoke, there was a note from Mack on the refrigerator saying I was to "Go nowhere. Make soup."

First I made breakfast: Nero Wolfe's recipe for griddle cakes with Mt. Tamalpais honey on top, strong coffee.

Make soup, eh? So that was the first order of the day. How was I to make soup if I was also constrained to go nowhere? Generally soup making was preceded by market going. Well, there was always beans. I always had beans on hand. Boy, I thought, as I forked the last of the pancakes, it would do me a world of good to build a minestrone. I had the pig pieces: bacon, sausage, and ham. I had beans and macaroni. I could always add the fresh vegetables later. I made a list of the ones I would want: cabbage, zucchini, celery, onion, fresh basil. Meanwhile I could get going on the base. But what was I making soup for? It wasn't Gramps' Night. Nor did I have a delivery due to The Splash for two days. Well, I would do what Mack said and ask questions later. I would be a model of obedience to Mack.

I made soup. Mindlessly I browned pig meats, washed beans, squeezed garlic, poured wine, poured broth from my stock pot, grabbed pulpy tomatoes from cans and mushed them in my hands, letting the juices dribble through my fingers to the soup. Hours passed.

Then Mack was standing in the kitchen doorway, smiling at me. "I think you made a good choice, not going to jail. You look good. Last night you were really wasted. A zombie."

"You know, Mack," I burst into talk, "for a minute there, it looked attractive, the idea of jail. Safe. A hidey hole. But then you said that about catching the Rapist and I felt so amazed. Well, not amazed exactly; I was too beat to feel anything that strong but I experienced a glimmer of life, something stirring in my soul. I felt . . . well, I guess what I must have felt was some kind of . . . hope. The idea captured my imagination . . . which had been running around so wild and loose." I looked searchingly at Mack, fearful now that it wasn't true, that he had just said it for my sake, to keep me going, while in truth it remained as always, hopeless. "I don't suppose you really meant it. There's no way in the world I could catch him . . ."

"Let me show you something."

I rinsed my hands, dried them, and followed Mack to the living room.

"Sit down."

I sat.

"Got something here I want to show you." He revealed a large manila envelope.

My heart pounded with excitement. "It's the blowup. I'd forgotten all about it."

"Yeah, it's the blowup all right."

This was it, I thought. Now I'll know everything. I can tell by Mack's face that I'll know. Will it be Ishmael? Louise? A strange black man? Or would it, even in the blowup, remain the shadowy figure of the Eternal Rapist?

Mack slid the picture from the envelope and passed it over to me, watching my face.

I gazed full upon it. Grainier and fuzzier though it was

from expanding the picture, the figure at the window had clarified, was recognizable. The blood rose to my face. "I . . . I don't get it," I said, because the figure was me.

"Remember, I made you that cup of tea with rum that night. Maybe you took a turn around the house after I left, then, because of the rum, forgot that you did that."

"Yes, that's right, I did wander out. I went to the window to see what Louise might have seen."

"That's another thing I want to tell you. She never came in that window. And the knife wasn't hers. It was Sam's. I asked him about it before he left. Remember how everything had gotten dumped out of his pack?"

"Yes, I do remember. Oh dear. What a mess. And what a disappointment. I had such hopes for this picture. Damn." I got up and paced about. "Before you showed me the picture, I had this flash that the figure might still be shadowy, that it would be the Eternal Rapist who's always there for us no matter what, always there behind the window for us women, always there," I pointed to Mack's breast, "on the other side of your bones, for you men. Lurking, skulking, a dark shadow, never to be identified or caught . . ."

"But then the Eternal Rapist turned out to be you."

"What?"

"You. You behind the window looking in. The Eternal Rapist, Ronda, is only a state of mind, and that's what you've got to come to grips with. You let him lodge so firmly in your imagination that your entire life began falling apart, culminating in that ridiculous act last night. You are going to have to stop losing control and shape up and the way you begin to do that is to admit that it was you behind that window."

"But . . . but there *is* a Rapist!"

"Yes. There is a man, a sick man in this town, who is terrifying women, causing their lives to disintegrate from fear. I've learned something about the power of that man from watching you. And I sympathize. And I realize that women all over town are going through what you are to one degree or another. Now we are going to do something about it."

"But what?"

"We'll start with Gramps' Night. Gramps called me yesterday, all upset that you'd canceled, let them down. I told him to come tonight and to bring as many old people as he could because I want to talk to them all." He got up to go. "I'll be back at seven."

"You're not going to tell me any more?"

"No. I'll tell you all at seven."

"Can I shop for vegetables?"

Mack stroked his chin, considering. "Yes."

"Can I go for a run?"

"No." He smiled. "And promise me that whenever a thought about the Rapist crosses your mind, you'll say to yourself, I'm going to catch him."

"I will. I'm going to do everything you tell me to."

2...

*I*t seemed like there were about fifty old people gathered at my house that night. We had to borrow some card tables from neighbors. When we'd polished off the minestrone and commenced on the various desserts, Mack addressed us all.

"First I want you to take a look at these." He removed a pile of stickers from a cardboard carton and passed them around. The sticker, which was round, showed an old lady looking through a telescope around which was spelled these words: This House Is Watched.

"I'm asking you to set up neighborhood watch committees. You all come from different parts of town. Neighborhood watch is a nice way of saying snoop. I want to set every soul in this town to snooping. I want you, individually, to set up meetings in your neighborhoods, give out these stickers for people to put on their doors and windows, and tell them all to get snooping on each other, night and day. At the smallest sign of anything suspicious, call the cops. I want people to illuminate their yards at night and move their dining room tables to a window where they can snoop during dinner. Make it a habit to watch the house next door. If you're out walking at night, carry a big flashlight and flash it all around. It makes a good weapon too. If *ever* you see, hear, smell, or suspect anything in the slightest out of the ordinary, call us.

"We don't care how many calls are false alarms. We can't be everywhere but you all can. People will say they don't want their privacy invaded. Tell them the alternative. Burglary is up fifty percent in this town. We've had murder for the first time in the town's history. And we've had rape. That Rapist has too much power. I now empower all of you to catch him. I speak to you first of all because you have more time on your hands to attend to this. You sleep less at night. You're curious, sharp-eyed, quick-witted . . ."

"Fast on our feet now, too," said one of them.

And they told Mack about the night at my house that they spotted, then nabbed, Joey Horgan.

"That's great," said Mack, "but I always want you to call the police—not try and apprehend any suspicious character yourself. I promise you we'll get there as fast as we can."

"But this is such a wonderful idea, Mack. Not only will you have the whole town on the watch but the stickers will be a potent deterrent in the same way those burglar alarm stickers are. Only better. An alarm can be dismantled but a prowler doesn't know where the snooper is. He could be watching him the very minute he's reading the sticker. I love it! By gum, we're going to catch that Rapist. He doesn't have a chance."

Everyone cheered. Mack handed out bags of stickers to

each Gramps'-Nighter and an outline of suggestions regarding the neighborhood meetings, points to bring up, how to organize.

I felt extremely moved as I looked around at my old people. They had the light of battle in their eyes. They felt needed and useful—which they were.

"Every Gramps' Night, report on your progress to Ronda, and she'll report to me. Remember, I expect to hear that police switchboard go crazy. Any more of those brownies?"

When the last old folk had gone out the door, I asked Mack if he'd stay the night again.

"You're still scared?"

"Not of the Rapist so much. I'm expunging him from my imagination pretty well, but I guess I'm still feeling a little emotionally frail. You see, there's this guy. . . ."

And I told him all about Joey Horgan. I showed Mack the other pictures Joey had taken and told him the whole story, ending with Joey's threat to come and live with me and finish the essay whether I wanted him to or not. "He's such a powerful personality, I feel I can't fight him. It's just too much for me on top of everything else." (I had yet to tell Mack about "everything else." Would I ever be able to?)

"Don't fight him, then."

"What?"

"Let him come."

"Why?"

"Yeah," Mack said musingly. "Let him come. He said he'll be quiet and not interfere with your life. It'll mean there's someone here with you—so you won't be so nervous. He's actually a well-known photographer. It'll probably be a great book. Just divorce yourself from it. You know it isn't you. It's only his vision of you. He's not taking anything from you. How could he? Only if you let yourself think he is. Again, it's all in the mind. You let yourself get upset too readily. I'll grant you life hasn't been easy for you lately, but . . . hell."

I stirred up the fire, threw on some sticks. "In a way it's a relief to give in to Joey and not feel I have to fight him about it, fight him and, in the end, lose, which I would. So I'll do what you say—embrace him."

"I don't think I said to do that."

"Just a figure of speech, the opposite of fight. Although I read recently that women who embrace cancer die of it faster than those who fight it tooth and nail." The fire crackled and hissed—a good sound. "It sure is hard to know how to live, Mack, to know how to be in the world. You're ahead of the game having a police uniform to wear. Are you sure you wouldn't let me keep yours, just to wear around the house sometimes when I need to?"

"I'm sure."

I sighed.

"I'll spend the night."

"Thanks." I went for the sleeping bag and pillow. "Any orders for tomorrow?"

"Stick around. Write a story about Neighborhood Watch Groups for the town and county papers. Then, when Maude's through work, she's coming over to see you with a business proposition."

"When do I get to run?"

"When I say so."

3 . . .

"*I* blame myself, Miss." Maude arrived around three o'clock the following afternoon. She went to my fridge for wine and poured herself a hefty goblet.

We went to the living room so she could put her feet up. She looked tired. It's hard to look with fresh eyes at an old friend, but it struck me that we weren't as young as we used to be, me and Maude, not as young as we were, say, in high school.

I remembered a time in our twenties when we were in a bar and the waitress said, "Can I see your I.D.?" and we both dove for our wallets. Maude glared at me and said, "She means *me*." She did too. That was the last time we, I mean *she* was asked. But to me Maude was more beautiful than ever. I wonder how I looked to her. We both, for sure, had been through a thing or two in the last decade.

"What do you mean you blame yourself?"

"That morning you came for coffee, after Sam left— God, was it only the day before yesterday?—I should have seen what a state you were in. Especially when you started writing those crazy notes all over the table. I mean, clearly you were going over the edge, and what did I do? I fanned the flames." She drank. "Fanned them! Instead of calming you down to make you see reason, I stir you up even more so that you go home and make that absolutely insane phone call to Louise accusing her of killing your dog!"

"How did you learn about that?"

"I'm coming to that in a moment. First I have to finish blaming myself. Sit down, we don't have to have a fire. I'm not staying that long . . ."

"I want one."

"It's about eighty degrees outside."

"I wouldn't know. Mack doesn't let me out."

"Anyhow," Maude continued, "all I did was fill you with more fear and add to your already irrational feelings about Louise who, mind you, *we don't even know.*"

"I'm just beginning to think I might have wronged her a little."

"Just a little. She comes to talk to you one night and you break her nose and call her the County Rapist. . . ."

I looked admiringly at my fire and threw a pillow down in front of it to sit on.

"But you weren't in any mood to get to know her that

night. You were in an overwrought state and you were prejudiced against her. You simply leaped to a wild conclusion. Also it's so satisfying to hate someone we subconsciously feel we have wronged. It eases our consciences to paint them as a bugabear."

"Bugabear! What a great word. Apropos."

"Now listen to this. Joe came in to see me after work today."

He'd said nothing, just stood there while Mack handcuffed me and dragged me away. He hadn't even watched me go. He'd just gone back into the house and closed the door. Probably he was missing something on the telly . . .

"He's furious. He's had it up to here with you. He says he's sick of feeling guilty about you and he just wants you to get the hell out of his life."

"Hold on a minute." Maude got up, went to the kitchen, returned with a replenished wineglass. This time she sat on the edge of the couch instead of lying down. "I explained to him that you'd simply had a slight breakdown but were currently on the mend and I promised he'd never see hide nor hair of you again. That took the wind out of his sails but not before he said he was prepared to swear out a warrant for your arrest if you came around his house again."

"He did? He said that? Joe?"

"Yes, he did. He said he'd already told you on the phone that day that he wished to sever all relations with you and recreate his marriage."

"Ah, so that's how you learned about my phone call. Yes. That's true, he did say that. Yes, he did. Right."

"Then we had a real cozy talk because he found me so receptive. He admitted he never could have lived with you. He couldn't stand your life-style, your casual housekeeping, your indifference to comfort . . ."

"My cat and my dog . . ."

"Your cat and your dog."

"Gramps' Night."

"He *hated* Gramps' Night."

"I knew all that, Maude. I knew it in my heart. But he should have said. He should have just told me. It would have made it easier, to just know."

"He wanted to be kind. He didn't want to hurt you even more. Anyhow, I said I'd exact a promise from you that you'd not bother them anymore. Louise is rather frightened of you now."

I tried not to feel pleased.

"You do understand that it's all over with you and Joe, and that Louise has been the wronged one all along."

Oh, Joe, I thought. Joe, my only love. As for Louise, how do I know for sure that she didn't murder Blue? And steal Moby and alter my pap smear and . . .

"Yes," I said obediently. "I understand."

4 . . .

"*B*ut wait a minute, Miss," I said as Maude was going out the door. "Mack said you had a business proposition for me,"

"That's right, I forgot." Maude came back in and sat down again but not before she'd refilled her glass to the brim.

"Do you think you're drinking too much these days?"

"Yes, I do. But that's because I'm so unhappy in my work. I'm about to change all that. I want to go to work for Ronda's Soup Service. You need a business manager."

"Boy, that's an understatement."

"Here's my proposition: you go on with your gardening and soup cooking. I'll go around and hit every restaurant in the county, getting orders, and I'll make deliveries. I'll even shop for you and go to the produce markets at dawn. We'll save that way. We split fifty-fifty."

"Deal."

"I'm going to ask you to give up one Gramps' Night. It's too much for you and it does eat into the profits. We're out to make a living wage, after all. You can make it up to them by giving them more running time. Running's much more important than eating. By the way, when are you running your next marathon?"

"Are you crazy? Never. I can't see any reason in the world to run a marathon more than once. There are certain things that don't bear repeating."

"Name another."

Rape, I thought, but couldn't say. If I couldn't say it to Maude, whom could I ever say it to? Please say it, I begged myself. Try.

I couldn't. My throat clenched.

"God," said Maude, "don't look so desperate. Well, I've really got to go. 'Bye partner."

My throat opened. I smiled. "I'm so glad we'll work together. I absolutely love having you and Mack tell me what to do. Teaching me how to live. It seems so simple after all. I wonder what all the fuss was about." I walked her out to her car. "I can't believe, Miss, that only two days ago I was practically certifiable."

"I can't believe that only two minutes ago I was turning into the town wino."

We laughed and hugged each other. Life! I thought. How sweet it is!

5 . . .

Joey Horgan didn't make an appearance until the next day. He found me washing clams for chowder, taking them in handfuls, holding them under the gushing faucet of the kitchen sink.

"Well, these pictures are a real disappointment," he said, tossing a pile down on the counter.

"What?" I said over the sound of the water.

"I didn't want to get your attention by using a flash so I opened the lens as far as I could but, hell, it was still nighttime and . . ."

"What?"

"Turn the fuckin' faucet off!" he shouted.

"No," I shouted back. "You said you wouldn't interfere with my life. You said you'd be like a tiny mouse. I'll turn the faucet off when I'm through washing these clams. Not before. Take a picture of me, why don't you?"

Joey looked astonished. Then he grinned.

When my clams were whistle clean, I addressed myself to the pictures. The man never ceased to amaze me. He'd gotten pictures of me in Mack's uniform!

"I hafta admit I got my hopes up when you and him stopped in front of the police station. I got this flash that you'd get busted and it'd be great publicity for the book."

"Oh yeah? How's that?"

"Well, think of all the saints who've been imprisoned. Not to mention writers. It coulda put you in their league. Like: O. Henry, Ezra Pound, Dashiell Hammett, Solzhenitsyn, de Sade. See what I mean?"

"What about Daniel Defoe, García Lorca, St. John of the Cross, Thoreau, Socrates . . ." I grinned. "Face!"

He grinned too. "Okay, let's boogie: Oscar Wilde, Eldridge Cleaver, Genêt, Bill Coffin, Dostoevski . . ."

"Emily Dickinson—although her imprisonment was self imposed. Maybe I could learn to like you, Joey," I said, because it had been fun tossing these names back and forth, "but . . . I don't think so."

"I just didn't see how I could work in the booking. I mean, hell, impersonating an officer? What the hell. That's not saintly or writerly. I'da lost my audience. What were you doing that night, anyhow? I can't figure you out."

I sighed. "Search me. But I think you should go ahead

and consider your audience lost. Scrap the whole idea."

"I admit I felt discouraged. I began to wonder who exactly I was dealing with here. I was confounded."

Joey did look rather despondent. I laughed. "If you want a saint in a police uniform, go across the street and meet Mack Scher. He is everything that is generous, gentle, and good. Moral too. An angel. If I were you, I'd sanctify Mack."

"Yeah, but you got a . . . a quality. It fascinates me. I think I'll go ahead with the essay."

"Very well, do whatever you want. I'm just going to make a clam chowder for my soup business."

Joey looked lost for words, He, like Joe, seemed to have had the wind taken out of his sails. It was probably hard for Joey to know what to say if he couldn't be obnoxious.

"Seems like you've changed."

"Thank you."

"Well, how come?"

"I'm burying my bugabears, Joey, or unburying them, I guess is more apt."

All but one, I thought. I had dug up the Eternal Rapist and was getting a good look at him. I was attacking the problem of the County Rapist with a full consciousness. But my own particular personal rape was deeply buried yet. I couldn't get it up to look at, let alone deal with. As my throat closed to speak of it, so did my mind strangle to think of it.

6 . . .

*M*aude's terrified voice came over the line. "There's a prowler in my yard right this minute."

It was almost a week later, Gramps' Night.

"Hush," I said to the old people. "It's Maude on the line. There's a prowler in her yard."

"Shall I call the cops?" I asked her.

"No. They've been called. I got a call from a neighbor-hood snoop who spotted him going over my fence, then called the police. I'm supposed to just act natural and not alarm him, so he'll still be here when they come. I figured it would help to hear your voice. Also I'm brushing my hair as I talk. Does that sound natural?"

"Real natural. Where are the kids?"

"Out. They're at their father's for the night."

"Hold on a minute." I reported to the party, "A neigh-borhood-watch person called Maude to tell her they'd seen this prowler and called the police. You see, it's working! Now she's trying to act natural so he'll stay there to be caught.

"Maude?"

"Yes, I'm still here. He's probably waiting for me to go to bed. If it's him. If it's the Rapist."

"Did you hear anything outside?"

"After I got the call, before I called you, I listened hard, but you know how it is—every little noise is him."

"Your windows are locked?"

"Yes."

"There's nothing to be scared about, then. The cops are on the way. Anyhow, Miss, it's probably not the Rapist. You're too old and too ugly." With all my heart I hoped that it was. Did Maude have bedposts? Yes, she did. Good.

"To think he might be looking in at me right now."

"Are you still brushing your hair?"

"Yes, my arm's getting exhausted. I'd rather be drink-ing wine. That's natural. Will you hold on while I get some wine?"

"Well, okay, but . . ."

I heard her set down the phone. I turned to call out to the yard the latest highlights and saw that all the Gramps'-Nighters were gone. Oh Lord. I'd have to go after them at once. "Maude?" She still wasn't back on the line. I whistled into the receiver to try to get her atention but my mouth had gone dry and it sounded more like a puff. Then I began to worry that something had gone amiss with her, or that the police had come and she'd forgotten me. I didn't want to hang up and desert her.

"Miss?" Ah, there she was.

"Thank goodness you're back. All the old folks have gone. I'm afraid they're going over to your house. They all think they're the New Centurions these days. I'd better go and stop them. Do you mind? Are you okay? I don't want any of them to get hurt."

"Go on. I'm okay. 'Bye."

Every damn one of them had set off for Maude's house three blocks away. I quickly passed the walkers, but the runners were well ahead. Spotlights from their flashes bobbed along the road before them. Overhead was a gibbous moon half-shrouded by clouds. "Hey, you guys, stop! We can't interfere with this. We don't want to frighten the prowler away. The police are coming, probably there now." I ran like hell, shouting anxiously at each of the posse as I passed until I reached Gramps at the front, to whom I repeated my dissuasions.

Gramps expostulated, "The police'll be coming from Miller Avenue. If he runs, he'll run this way. He might git away."

"Right," I said, humoring him. "Then let's stop right here and form a cordon. We'll make a wall of ourselves and if we hear anyone running this way, we'll hit him with the flashlights—first with the light from them, then, if necessary, with the torches themselves."

"We'll batter the bejesus out of him."

The stragglers had caught up and formed a knot around us. We told them the plan and they strung out in a line across the dark street that tunneled toward Maude's house under a canopy of sycamores. We doused our lights and fell remarkably silent. I looked at my line of vigilantes and felt so proud of them. A more misshapen, ancient, gargoylish contingent couldn't be imagined, especially in the weird light of the veiled moon. We looked like something out of a tapestry by Heironymus Bosch, without his color and charm. I began to hope the Rapist would run this way—smack into this cordon of bugabears and boogeypersons. To encounter anything so unexpected and nightmarishly horrible as we were could cause a cardiac arrest as well as a police one and save the expense of trial and punishment.

My heart stopped as I heard running footsteps, panting. A shadowy figure appeared at the end of the street, then was suddenly illuminated from behind. "Stop or we'll shoot!" the police shouted.

He kept running. "Lights!" I yelled, for if they shot we'd be right in the line of fire.

On went the old folks' flashlights, hitting the fugitive like something palpable, a bludgeon of light. He stopped and cowered, literally cowered before us, this scourge of the town and county, subdued by lights that were held in the mottled, wrinkled, gnarled, parchmentlike, veined, knotted, arthritic, trembling hands of the town's aged.

He was apprehended, seized, and cuffed. He was disarmed of a knife. Around his waist was a rope. He was a black man, dressed in black. I got as near as I could. I wanted to see this Rapist. I wanted to see his face, his eyes. If only . . . if only I could see something there that would help me understand.

But I looked in vain. He was just a man. Anybody. His eyes were just eyes—anybody's eyes.

The Lone-Juicing, Uncowed Runner-of-Mountains, Female

1 . . .

For me and Mack and Maude, there was much rejoicing all the next month. Daily my spirits lifted until I couldn't remember my unhappiness of the fall and winter and spring.

Joey, although his essay was completed, still spent nights on what he called my torture rack—the studio couch in the living room—and he came and went much in the way that Moby had used to do. He was quite a lot like Moby. I still had the nagging feeling that I could get to like him in time—in maybe a couple of hundred years.

Our soup service throve. Maude was a wonderful help. It looked like she and Mack were getting rather fond of one another.

I wrote a good story. My creative juices were torrential. As well, I had sold a story to the *New Yorker*, every fictionist's dream, and to offset the possible attendant feeling of my art becoming entombed in that periodical, I also sold a story to a pulp magazine, *Fantasy and Science Fiction*.

It was three weeks before Mack let me run again. It turned out he had slyly determined that a ban on my running would gain me some weight as well as keep me under his thumb. The day came when he pronounced me "a little less wraithlike" and dispatched me to the mountain. A good thing too. I was getting awfully restless.

It was fine to be back on the trails. I ran. I leaped, and whirled and skipped. I walked, drinking in all the good mountain sights and smells. We were now in the heart of summer. The grassy hills were turned to gold. The creeks no longer rushed or cataracted; they meandered. The flowers were gone but the huckleberries were fruiting. The shy, sensitive does were followed by morbidly shy and sensitive fawns. The hawks and vultures circled inexorably, their predatory quests the same as any other season.

Yes, it was summer, and it wouldn't be long at all now until my boy, Sam, would be back from the YCC to spend a month at home.

I must have covered sixteen miles of trails on that mountain reunion that was a return to the fullness of life for me and coming to a new feeling of strength of heart and mind, of being almost indomitable.

2 . . .

*B*ut what of Ishmael? Oh yes, Ishmael.

I never heard one word from him after the night of his rape of me. I never saw him anywhere around town, although it was true I didn't go about much but stayed home making soup, gardening, and writing.

Then, one day at the library, I found myself getting out the big green volume of the California Penal Code and I realized I'd begun to allow myself to think about that night. I turned to "Rape."

"Rape is an act of sexual intercourse accomplished with a female, not the wife of the prepetrator, under either of the following circumstances."

Of the following circs, only the first two might apply to me that night: "1. Where she is incapable through lunacy or other unsoundness of mind, whether temporary or permanent, of giving legal consent. 2. Where she resists but her resistance is overcome by force or violence."

My mind had been unsound that night, especially if one cited my behavior later on. Pretty loony. I'd told Ishmael how emotionally frail I was feeling, that I wanted to be friends. I was incapable all right, but capable enough to say yes or no, legally or otherwise, and I'd said no, I'd resisted, and that's where the force had come in.

"The essential guilt of rape," the penal code went on to say, "consists in the outrage to the person and feelings of the female." Yes, I liked that. The person and feelings are outraged. That is nice language, a good description. "Any sexual penetration, however slight, is sufficient, to complete the crime where she is prevented from resisting by threats of great and immediate bodily harm accompanied by apparent power of execution."

Rape was a felony carrying a penalty of a year in the county jail or two to six years in the state pen, according to the discretion of the court.

I couldn't help but be struck by the fact that in this state of mine, the penalty for rape was not very much more severe than the penalty I would have suffered, if prosecuted, for letting the air out of Joe's tires.

3 . . .

As the days passed and I felt stronger, I began to think more about Ishmael and about what had transpired between us that night. He had said I'd be sorry. It emerged that I was feeling sorry. For him. I had a vision that because of what he'd done, he had, as promised, finally hung it up and become a monk. That he was off in some hut somewhere, fasting, praying, scourging himself. Indeed it seemed to me to be a grievous and sorrowful vision if it were so.

I knew now I would not report him for what he had done, would not ever speak of it to anyone. I knew, too, that this was wrong of me, that I had fallen into the trap of so many women I'd discovered in my "rape readings" who, especially, could not bring themselves to report acquaintance rape, somehow taking the blame on themselves, because they had a kind of relationship with the man, being more willing to forgive because they knew him, however slightly. I saw all this, saw that it was wrong and perhaps deluded of me and yet the fact remained, probably because I was feeling so good now myself, that I felt intensely sorry for Ishmael. I didn't want him to suffer. I wanted to forgive him. I wanted him to contend with life as I was doing.

4 . . .

O ne day I was in a new health-food restaurant sitting alone in a booth, reading *The Autobiography of Benjamin Franklin*, whom I was perhaps going to take for my new role model, St. Francis not having served me too well, when my attention was caught, held, fixed, by a voice coming from the booth behind me. The backs of the booths were head high and I would have had to stand and turn to see into that booth but I didn't need to. I recognized the voice. And as I listened, I felt those fine hairs of mine stand up on my body as they had not done for some time, although it was not from terror so much as horror, the same kind of cowering horror the County Rapist must have felt that night coming upon the Bosch-like cordon of the totally unexpected, something the mind can't grasp at once—the brain founders, the body cowers before what seems supernatural in its sudden, undreamed-of manifestation. Hearing this voice in the booth beyond, I felt as a skin diver once described feeling upon his first encounter with a shark. That feeling of being up against incarnate evil, in evil's own element, in evil's own time and space. The modern world no longer existed or was of any use to him. It was only him and this primeval creature in waters of millenniums ago.

This is what I heard:

"And you haven't fallen into the promiscuity pit?"

"No," came a sweet voice. "No, I have strong religious feelings that prevent me from that."

"You're a good woman. Unusual. Really unusual. Serene. I, too, have strong religious feelings. I'm considering joining a monastery but it's a big decision. What do you think?"

"Oh, I think it's wonderful!"

" . . . dedicate myself to God."

"Yes, yes. In my religion, Vedanta . . ."

He let her tell about her religion, then said soulfully, "The passions of the flesh hamper the growth of the spirit . . ."

My ears were ringing. I thought I would faint. I could not believe what I was hearing. I put my head down on the table, cradled in my arms. My head reeled as I considered all the ramifications of Ishmael's behavior and realized how he could go on like this forever, possibly disturbed enough not to understand what he was doing—or possibly knowing exactly, orchestrating the whole thing to a hair's breadth.

I believe I lost consciousness for a moment. "Are you all right?" the waiter inquired, touching my shoulder.

"What? Oh, yes." I jumped up. They were gone. I threw down some money for my meal and ran out the door. I saw them a block away, in the town square, my old arena.

I ran. I ran so fast that people stopped in their tracks

and stared. I passed by them like a specter, an Olympic-caliber blur.

The square had its usual complement of people, criss-crossing to the stores, waiting for the bus at the depot, the bums and burnouts in their own staked-out territory near the bank.

I ran like a fury until I got to Ishmael and the girl, who looked about sixteen years old. I skidded to a stop and laid hands on him. "You're under arrest!" I said.

"What! What are you doing? Get your hands off me."

He made as if to shrug me off but I held on for dear life, an absolute death grip. Then he struggled and tried to run but I grappled him to me with hoops of steel. I hung on with all the weight of my wraithlike form and of my outraged person and feelings.

"This man is a rapist," I said to his companion and to the townspeople forming curiously around us. "I am performing a citizen's arrest. Don't let him get away. Someone get a policeman."

"Let go of me. You're nuts. This woman is nuts. The whole town knows you're nuts," he said to me. And then, in spite of himself he said, "You'll never make it stick."

"Perhaps not, but I'll make it sticky for you. It will give you pause. You're under arrest," I said loudly, smiling now, loving the sound of it. I didn't need a uniform after all to be strong, able, effective. Wow, what a woman I was! "This man is a rapist," I said again in case some persons had missed it the first and second times around. "It's a citizen's arrest I'm performing here."

"She's nuts," Ishmael said. "This is Ronda Thompson. She's nuts."

I hoped the police would come soon. We could go on forever like this—him saying I'm nuts, me saying he's a rapist, every time a new person joined the group.

"She *is* nuts," I heard some people say. "She became unhinged when her lover left her—oh, six or eight months ago. Since then . . ."

When Ishmael's arrest was accomplished and he was booked, I swaggered out of the police station, across the square, and into the town tavern.

Well, I thought, taking a stool, we've caught the County Rapist and my personal rapist; only one to go, the big one, and that may take years—generations!

"What'll it be?"

"Boysenberry apple."

"On the rocks?"

"Straight up."

I sat alone. No one approached me although I could sense people looking in and talking about me—how I was a writer, a soupist, a runner, and a rapee—and crazier than a hoot owl.

But no one approached—probably because I looked too sinister. It was as if I had a magnetic field around me, not to mention my halo. . . .